SPARE CHANGE

THE SPENSER NOVELS

Hundred-Dollar Baby

School Days

Cold Service

Bad Business

Back Story

Widow's Walk

Potshot

Hugger Mugger

Hush Money

Sudden Mischief

Small Vices

Chance

Thin Air

Walking Shadow

Paper Doll

Double Deuce

Pastime

Stardust

Playmates

Crimson Joy

Pale Kings and Princes

Taming a Sea-Horse

A Catskill Eagle

Valediction

The Widening Gyre

Ceremony

A Savage Place

Early Autumn

Looking for Rachel Wallace

The Judas Goat

Promised Land

Mortal Stakes

God Save the Child

The Godwulf Manuscript

THE JESSE STONE NOVELS

High Profile

Sea Change

Stone Cold

Death in Paradise

Trouble in Paradise

Night Passage

THE SUNNY RANDALL NOVELS

Blue Screen

Melancholy Baby

Shrink Rap

Perish Twice

Family Honor

ALSO BY ROBERT B. PARKER

Appaloosa

Double Play

Gunman's Rhapsody

All Our Yesterdays

A Year at the Races
    (with Joan H. Parker)

Perchance to Dream

Poodle Springs
    (and Raymond Chandler)

Love and Glory

Wilderness

Three Weeks in Spring
    (with Joan H. Parker)

Training with Weights
    (with John R. Marsh)

SPARE CHANGE

ROBERT B. PARKER

G. P. PUTNAM'S SONS
New York

G. P. PUTNAM'S SONS
Publishers Since 1838
Published by the Penguin Group
Penguin Group (USA) Inc., 375 Hudson Street, New York, New York 10014, USA ·
Penguin Group (Canada), 90 Eglinton Avenue East, Suite 700, Toronto, Ontario M4P 2Y3,
Canada (a division of Pearson Penguin Canada Inc.) · Penguin Books Ltd, 80 Strand,
London WC2R 0RL, England · Penguin Ireland, 25 St Stephen's Green, Dublin 2, Ireland
(a division of Penguin Books Ltd) · Penguin Group (Australia), 250 Camberwell Road,
Camberwell, Victoria 3124, Australia (a division of Pearson Australia Group Pty Ltd) ·
Penguin Books India Pvt Ltd, 11 Community Centre, Panchsheel Park, New Delhi–110 017,
India · Penguin Group (NZ), 67 Apollo Drive, Rosedale, North Shore 0745, Auckland,
New Zealand (a division of Pearson New Zealand Ltd) · Penguin Books (South Africa) (Pty) Ltd,
24 Sturdee Avenue, Rosebank, Johannesburg 2196, South Africa

Penguin Books Ltd, Registered Offices:
80 Strand, London WC2R 0RL, England

Library of Congress Cataloging-in-Publication Data

Parker, Robert B., date.
Spare change / Robert B. Parker.
p.   cm.
ISBN 978-0-399-15425-6 (acid-free paper)
1. Randall, Sunny (Fictitious character)—Fiction. 2. Women private investigators—
Massachusetts—Boston—Fiction. 3. Boston (Mass.)—Fiction. I. Title.
PS3566.A686S59   2007   2007003137
813'.54—dc22

Printed in the United States of America
1   3   5   7   9   10   8   6   4   2

This book is printed on acid-free paper. ∞

BOOK DESIGN BY AMANDA DEWEY

This is a work of fiction. Names, characters, places, and incidents either are the product of the
author's imagination or are used fictitiously, and any resemblance to actual persons, living or
dead, businesses, companies, events, or locales is entirely coincidental.

While the author has made every effort to provide accurate telephone numbers and Internet addresses at the time of publication, neither the publisher nor the author assumes any responsibility for errors, or for changes that occur after publication. Further, the publisher does not have
any control over and does not assume any responsibility for author or third-party websites or
their content.

For Joan: once in a lifetime

SPARE CHANGE

I sat with my father at the kitchen table and looked at the old crime-scene photographs. Four men and three women, each shot behind the right ear. Each with a scatter of three coins near their head as they lay on the ground. There was in the implacable crime-scene photography no sense of lives suddenly extinguished, fear suddenly snuffed, no smell of gunshot or sound of pain. Just some dead bodies. The pictures were accurate and inclusive, but they distanced me from the subject. I didn't know if it was me or the process. Paintings didn't do it.

"The Spare Change Killer," I said.

My father grunted. "Papers liked that name," he said.

"Because of the coins, we thought at first maybe the perp was a panhandler, you know? 'Spare change'? And when the guy starts to give him some, the killer pops him and he drops the coins."

"Pops him in the back of the head?" I said.

"Yeah, that sort of bothered us, too," my father said. "But you know how it goes. You got something like this, you try out every theory you can."

"I remember this," I said.

"Yeah, you were about twelve," my father said, "when it started. And maybe fifteen when it was over."

"My memory was of how much you weren't home," I said.

My father nodded.

"And then it just stopped," I said.

My father nodded again.

"And you never caught him," I said.

My father shook his head.

"Maybe this time," he said.

"You think it's the same guy?" I said.

"Don't know," my father said. "Same bullet behind the ear. Same spare change on the ground."

"Same gun?"

"No."

"Doesn't mean much," I said. "He could certainly have acquired another gun."

"There were different guns in the first go-round," my father said. "Spare Change said he liked to experiment."

"He wrote you," I said.

"Regularly."

"You specifically?" I said.

"I was the head of the task force," my father said. "FBI, State, Boston Homicide."

"God," I said. "I didn't even remember that there was a task force."

"You were pretty much caught up in puberty at the time," my father said.

"Boys were pretty much everything I was interested in," I said.

"But now?"

"The boys are older," I said.

My father shrugged.

"Progress, I guess," he said.

"Why were you in charge?" I said.

"First two murders were in my precinct," my father said. "Plus, of course, I was the very paradigm of law-enforcement perfection."

"Oh," I said. "Yes, that, too."

"Since I retired," my father said, "I been reading a lot. Even books with big words. I been dying to say *paradigm.*"

"I'm proud to call you Daddy," I said.

He took a big manila envelope from a pile on the table and opened it. He took out a crime-scene photo and a letter, and put them on the table in front of me. The photograph was just like the other crime-scene photos. In this case a young black man was sprawled on the ground, facedown. There was a dark spill of blood around his head. A nickel, a dime, and a quarter lay in the blood.

"The new one?" I said.

"Yes," my father said. "Read the letter."

The letter said:

Hi, Phil,

You miss me? I got bored, so I thought I'd reestablish our relationship. Give us both something to do in our later years. Stay tuned.

Spare Change

It was neatly printed in block letters on plain white printer paper by someone probably using a fine-point Sharpie.

"Sounds like him?" I said.

"Yes."

"Anything from the paper, or the ink, or the handwriting?"

"Nothing from the paper and ink. Possibly the same handwriting. Block printing is hard. Probably right-handed."

"You'd guess that from the shot being behind the vic's right ear," I said.

"You would."

"So there's nothing to say this isn't the same guy."

"No," my father said. "I tried to keep his letters to me out of the papers, but I couldn't. The case was too hot. Some cluck in the mayor's office released them."

"So anyone could copycat it," I said.

"It's not a complicated writing style," my father said.

"You're back in this?" I said.

"Yes. They've asked me to consult. Even gave me a budget."

"And you want to do this?" I said.

"Yes," my father said.

I nodded and didn't say anything.

"And I want you to help me," my father said.

"Because?"

"You were a cop. You're smart. You're tough. You're pretty." My father grinned at me. "You, too, are a paradigm of law-enforcement perfection, and you're my kid."

I looked at him across the flat, deadly photographs. He was a thick, squat man with big hands that always made me think of a stonemason.

"Because I'm pretty?" I said.

"You get that from me," he said. "Will you help?"

"Daddy," I said, "I'm flattered to be asked."

I t was Monday morning. My bed was made; the kitchen
counters gleamed. I had applied makeup carefully, taken a
lot of time with my hair. The loft had been vacuumed and
dusted, and there were flowers on the breakfast table. I was
wearing embroidered jeans so tight that I'd had to lie down
to put them on. My top was a white tee that drifted off one
shoulder. I'd been doing power yoga with a trainer, and I was
happy with the way my shoulders looked. My shoes were
black platform sneakers that bridged the gap between casual
and dressy in just the right way. Richie brought Rosie back
from her weekend visit on Monday mornings, and it takes a

lot of work to look glamorous when you are trying very hard to look as if you aren't trying to look glamorous.

When they arrived I was casually painting under my skylight while the sun was good, and had been for a good five minutes. I put the brush down and picked Rosie up when she came in, and kissed her on the nose while she squirmed and wagged her tail and let me know simultaneously that she was thrilled to see me and wanted to be put down. I put her on the floor.

"Place looks great," Richie said.

"Oh," I said. "Thanks."

"You do, too."

I smiled.

"Oh," I said. "Thanks."

Richie put a paper bag on the breakfast table next to the flowers.

"What's in there?" I said.

"Coffee," Richie said, "and some corn and molasses muffins."

"Did you have in mind sharing?" I said.

"Sure," Richie said.

He opened the bag and took out two big paper cups of coffee and four muffins.

"Corn and molasses," I said. "My total fave."

Rosie went to her water dish and drank loudly and at length. I sat at the counter with Richie and picked up a muffin.

"Did my kumquat have a good time?" I said to Richie.

"She did."

"Did she go for walks?"

"Yes. We took her out every day on the beach."

"*We* being you and the wife."

Richie nodded.

"Kathryn," Richie said.

I nodded.

"And she likes Rosie?"

"She does."

"Where does Rosie sleep when she's there?" I said.

"In bed with me and Kathryn," Richie said.

He had taken the plastic cap off his coffee cup.

"And she doesn't mind?"

"Kathryn? Or Rosie?" Richie said.

"Not Rosie," I said.

"Kathryn doesn't mind," Richie said. "Love me, love my dog."

"Our dog," I said.

"I get her two weekends a month," Richie said. "I think it's clear that she's not mine exclusively."

"I know. I'm sorry."

Richie nodded. He was physically well organized. Maybe six feet tall. Strong-looking. Very neat. He always looked like he'd just shaved and showered. His thick, black hair was short. All his movements seemed precise and somehow integrated. He had a lot of the interiority that my father had. We ate some of our muffins and drank some of our coffee. Rosie eventually finished her water and came over and sat on the floor between us.

"Do you suppose all bull terriers drink water like that?" I said.

"I think it's some kind of 'glad to see you' ritual," Richie said. "She does it when she first gets to my house, too."

"Remember when we first got her?" I said.

"Right after we were married," Richie said.

"She was about the size of a guinea pig," I said.

"Maybe not that small," Richie said.

"And we had to be so careful of her at first so as not to roll over on her in bed."

We were both quiet.

"You okay?" Richie said after a time.

"Sure," I said. "You?"

"Yeah," Richie said. "I'm fine."

We drank some coffee and ate some muffin.

"Felix says he gave you a hand with something a while back."

I nodded.

"As far as your Uncle Felix goes, I'm still part of the family."

"Felix likes who he likes," Richie said. "Circumstance doesn't have much effect on him."

"I assume that he also dislikes who he dislikes," I said.

"He does," Richie said. "It is much better to be one of the ones he likes."

"I understand that," I said.

Richie broke off an edge of his second muffin and ate it.

"Felix says you had something going with a police chief on the North Shore," Richie said.

"I did," I said.

"And?"

"Now I don't."

"What was the problem?" Richie said.

"He was still hung up on his former wife," I said.

Richie nodded. He drank some coffee and put the cup down and smiled at me.

"You understand that?"

"Yes," I said. "I do."

Richie nodded, slowly looking at the surface of the coffee in his cup.

"I understand it, too," Richie said.

"Time now," I said, "for a pregnant silence."

"And then chitchat about Rosie some more," Richie said.

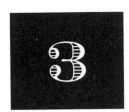

loved my father. My sister and I had competed with my mother for his attention all our lives. I was thrilled to have him sharing space with me. To be working with him on something important was a kind of victory. It was also odd.

They had an office for him at police headquarters. But he spent a lot of time in my loft. He was on the phone a lot. He was in and out a lot. At the end of the day, we usually had a drink together before he went home. I looked forward to the drink. And I looked forward to his going home.

On a bright, perfect Tuesday morning in early July he called me at seven-thirty, just after I came back from walking Rosie.

"I'll pick you up at eight," he said. "There's been another one."

The body had been found in among some tall reeds beside the Muddy River in the Back Bay Fens. It was a man, maybe fifty-five, wearing a powder-blue jogging suit and brand-new white sneakers. He'd been shot behind the right ear. There were three coins beside his head. The Boston Homicide commander was there, a big, tough, well-dressed man named Quirk. There were a dozen other cops, and half a dozen members of the press, including two television people.

"Phil," Quirk said.

"Martin," my father said. "This is my daughter Sunny."

"Captain," I said.

We shook hands.

"So far," Quirk said, "it's same-o same-o. Wallet is still with him, a hundred and twenty dollars in it. There's no sign of sexual activity. No evidence of any assault except the gunshot that killed him. Haven't, obviously, got the bullet yet. But from the look of the wound, there's nothing unusual about the weapon."

My father was looking down at the man. He squatted and pushed blood-stiffened hair aside to look at the wound.

"A nine, maybe," he said. "Or a .38."

"Sure," Quirk said. "Maybe a .40. It didn't exit his skull. So the ME will tell us."

"And then what will we know," my father said.

"Nothing much," Quirk said. "But we should be used to that by now."

My father nodded.

"Do a walk-through yet?" he said.

"Yeah," Quirk said. "I'll have one of the crime-scene guys take you through it."

The crime-scene guy was a young woman with copper-colored hair, which she wore in a ponytail. We stood with her on the sidewalk near Park Drive. Her name was Emily.

"Perp must have followed him in here," Emily said.

She stepped onto a barely discernible path that led toward the reeds and the river. Daddy and I followed her.

"He had some scissors with him," Emily said, "and a shopping bag, with half a dozen cut weeds in it. We figure he was getting himself stuff for some kind of floral arrangement."

We paused next to some truncated weed stalks.

"This is where he was cutting the reeds," Emily said. "Already matched them with the ones in the bag. He was probably going to cut some more, because he still had the scissors in his hand when he was shot. They landed a few feet away from him when he went down."

"And he didn't go down here," I said.

"No."

Emily led us along the slight path.

"He moved on, looking for just the right reed," Emily said. "Down here."

We were at the crime scene.

"He found the right reed," Emily said. "He stopped, started to cut it, and the perp . . ."

Emily pretended to shoot with her forefinger and thumb.

"Bang, bang," Emily said.

"Twice?" Daddy said.

Emily almost blushed.

"No. Excuse me," Emily said. "I was just dramatizing. As far as we can tell now, it was one and out."

My father didn't say anything.

"Footprints?" I said.

Emily shook her head.

"Ground's marshy," Emily said. "And doesn't hold a print. Even if it did, people come in here all the time. Smoke dope. Drink. Have sex. Cut reeds. Look at birds."

"What's his name?" Daddy said.

Emily pulled a small notebook from her shirt pocket and opened it.

"Eugene Nevins," Emily said. "Lives on Jersey Street. He's wearing a wedding ring. No one answers his phone, it's his voice on the answering machine, and the apartment listing is his name only."

"Widowed or divorced, maybe," my father said.

"Gay maybe," I said. "Not a ton of straight men out cutting reeds for a floral arrangement."

My father nodded.

"Any next of kin?"

"Not yet," Emily said. "We're looking."

"When did it happen?" Daddy said.

"We'll know better after they get him onto the table," Emily said. "We're guessing five, six, seven o'clock yesterday evening."

"No one heard a gunshot."

"No one reported one," Emily said. "Lot of traffic noise all around the Fenway that hour. Summer day everyone's got the windows closed, a/c on."

"You could probably fire off a handgun in Quincy Market at noon, and no one would report a gunshot," my father said.

"It doesn't sound like they think it does," Emily said.

"And they don't want what they heard to be a gunshot," Daddy said. "They got other things to do."

"Emily," I said. "How cynical does that sound?"

"Captain Randall has earned the right to it, ma'am."

"Yes," I said. "I guess he has."

osie and I were both fed and walked for the night. She was asleep on the bed with her paw over her nose, half under a pillow. I was beside her in my pajamas, reading photocopies of letters that the Spare Change Killer had sent to my father twenty years ago.

Dear Captain Randall,

First, congratulations on being named to head the Spare Change Task Force. It's a nice name, "the Spare Change Killer." I like it. And after only two events. Don't fret. There will be more. Wouldn't want you to get bored (ha, ha). Do

you wonder why I always leave some change at an event?
That's for me to know and you to find out, isn't it?
    Good hunting,
    Spare Change

It was laborious block printing, as if the letters were drawn rather than written.

Dear Phil,

    You don't mind if I call you Phil, I hope, now that we've begun to establish a relationship. I know you think of me often, as I do likewise of you. I wonder if we'll ever meet? Of course, it's always possible that we have met and you don't know it. You know what they always say, Phil, it's a small world. Anyway, how's the investigation going? I like how hard you are working on establishing a pattern. I'm sorry to tell you that from my end, you don't seem to be getting anywhere.

    Let's stay in touch.
    SC

Beside me Rosie snored softly. The overhead lights were off. I was reading in the small circumference of my bedside lamp. The rest of the loft was dark. The only real sound in the loft was Rosie and the soft rush of the air-conditioning. But the sound of the disingenuous voice from twenty years ago seemed to have materialized in the silence and the darkness. It hung in the air of my loft as if I could actually hear it.

Dear Phil,

How are you doing? As I guess you know, I'm doing quite well. The last event was especially good. It's fun to get them totally unaware. Walking along and then pow! Dead. You suppose that is why I do this, Phil? For the fun of seeing them go down? I bet you'd like to know that. Maybe I don't even know it . . . or maybe I do. I'll be looking for you on the television.

Be good. (Not like me, huh?)
SC

I put my hand on Rosie's flank as she slept beside me. She was warm and solid. I kept my hand on her as I read the rest of the letters. When I was done, I picked up the new letter and reread it. Same block printing. Same voice. Same person? No way to know. Several of the letters had been published in the papers twenty years ago. Anyone who cared to could find them and mimic them. Or the recent one could be authentic, the simpleminded voice connected to the block printing. The way it was written influenced how it sounded. Form and content? I should have paid more attention in freshman comp. Maybe I could find a forensics English teacher.

I put the letters on the floor, and shut off my reading lamp, and lay on my back looking into the darkness, and tried to think obliquely about what I'd read, as if maybe I'd see better if I didn't look right at it.

No point in trying to think about the old murders. No one had solved them in twenty years. Focus on the new ones. I'm Spare Change.

I'm walking around the city with a loaded gun. It's much heavier when it's loaded. I see somebody I want to kill. Do I follow the person? Waiting for my chance? Do I walk up behind the person and pull the trigger without a word? I shoot him only once. I know what I'm doing. I'm confident he's dead. I put the gun away. I put the coins down. Do I linger and watch from someplace? Do I get a kick out of seeing the body discovered? Watching the cops arrive? Or do I walk away without another glance. Get my enjoyment from the newspaper accounts. The television stand-ups with the crime scene in the background. "Glamour-puss TV person reporting live . . ." Do I do this for the publicity? To feel important? Why write to Daddy? Why the beloved adversary crap? All the murders, the two new ones, the earlier seven, had in common was that they were done in places where they could be done covertly. I have never broken in to any place and shot someone. I have always been outdoors, in the city, near the public but out of sight. Along the river. Under an overpass. Down an alley. In a public parking garage. Is that how I pick my victims? Wait around in a good place to shoot, and wait for someone to wander by? Or did I preselect on some obscure basis and follow them around until they went someplace where I could shoot them unobserved?

I was right back to why. *Why does Spare Change do it? Why leave the coins? They're not always the same denomination of coins, but always three of them. And why now? After twenty years. If it was the same guy, what caused him to stop? And what caused him to start again? What if it was a copycat? What set him off? Or her. Most serial killers were men. But it didn't have to be a man.*

My eyes had adapted to the darkness, and I could see the

outlines of my home. My easel under the skylight. My table and chairs in the bay. My kitchen counter. My silent television. Rosie was small and substantial beside me. My gun was where it always was at night, in the drawer of my bedside table.

We met in a big room in the mayor's office at Boston City Hall. From the outside, Boston City Hall looks like Stonehenge rising in massive isolation in the middle of a big, empty brick plaza. Inside is less welcoming: gray slab stone and harsh light, as if somehow the building were more important than its function.

The mayor was a much more human presence than the building. He presided quite genuinely over the meeting, just as if it wasn't taking place in a misplaced Gothic castle. The police commissioner was there, and Captain Quirk, and the head of State Police Homicide, Captain Healy. The Commissioner of Public Safety was there, and a man named Nathan

Epstein, who was Special Agent in Charge of the Boston FBI office. There was a woman from the Suffolk County DA's office, and a guy from the AG. There were also assistants and associates of all of these high-ranking people, plus my father, plus his assistant, which was me.

"As you speak," the mayor said, "please identify yourselves. I don't want to waste time now with introductions, and I don't know if everyone knows everyone."

He looked around the room. No one objected. The mayor nodded once.

"We'll keep a record of the meeting," he said. "But it will be a private record for our own information. We're not going to succeed with the Spare Change killings without a free and uninhibited flow of information. So forget turf. And don't worry about how it sounds. We have a common goal. Hell, a common need. So I urge you to speak freely, and, if I may, I urge you not to bullshit me. Or each other."

The mayor looked at the Boston Police commissioner.

"Beth Ann," he said, "why don't you start."

She was a lean woman in a tailored gray suit. Her eyes were pale blue. Her hair was verging on gray. She wore a wedding ring.

"Beth Ann Hartigan," she said. "Boston Police commissioner. We've been getting good cooperation from our friends at the state level, and from the federal government as well."

She nodded at Epstein.

"We have increased police presence on the streets of Boston by a third. We have supplemented our own resources with state officers and federal marshals."

"Is it a visible presence?" the mayor said.

"That is our hope, but I don't know. I think to make the public fully comfortable we'd have to flood the city with far more men and women than we have, than all of us have."

The mayor nodded.

"Well, the public will perceive what it perceives," he said. "There are more police persons looking for the killer?"

"Yes," Hartigan said. "The absolute maximum number we can pull together."

"How about the progress of the investigation?" the mayor said.

"Captain Quirk is in charge of that for us," Hartigan said. "I'll ask him to address that."

The mayor looked at Quirk.

"Go ahead, Captain," the mayor said.

"Martin Quirk, Boston Homicide commander. *Progress* is too strong a word. We've put together a pretty good team to chase this guy down. Special Agent Epstein from the FBI. Captain Healy from State Homicide. Phil Randall, who was in charge of the original case, has come out of retirement to consult for us. Epstein has provided us a profile from the FBI—tells us the killer is a white male, between twenty and forty-five, some education but nothing advanced or specialized. Couple years of college maybe."

"How do they know that?" the mayor said.

"Place where he did the crimes. Language he uses in his letters to the police."

Quirk looked at Epstein.

"Maybe a little guessing."

Epstein smiled and shrugged.

"And?" the mayor said.

"And we're nowhere," Quirk said. "We don't know who he is. We don't know why he does it."

"What about the coins?" the mayor said.

"They may be just to tag the crime," Quirk said. "Let us know it's him, something nonincriminating, so if he got picked up and we found change in his pocket it wouldn't mean anything. Most people have change on them."

The mayor nodded.

"Or," Quirk said, "it may be just something he does to confuse us, and there is no meaning to the coins. Or it may mean something really important to him, but it doesn't mean anything to anyone else."

"Have you had any forensic psychiatry input?" the mayor said.

"Yes."

"And?"

Quirk shook his head.

"He kills for reasons we don't understand," Quirk said. "We don't know why he did it twenty years ago. If it's the same guy. We don't know why he stopped. We don't know why it's started again."

The mayor looked at my father.

"Phil?" he said.

"Phil Randall," my father said. "I got nowhere with it first time out. I thought then, and I still think, that what will eventually happen is he'll make a mistake. He'll choose the wrong place to do the shooting, and someone will spot him during the commission. Or his gun will jamb and the vic will ID him. Or one of us will get lucky and walk in on him in the act."

"What we are going to do," Quirk said, "is flood the next crime scene, try to seal it off, if it's someplace where we can, in the hopes that maybe he hangs around to watch."

"Do you think he might?" the mayor said.

"FBI profilers think he might," Quirk said. "Our shrinks think he might."

"How will you know him?"

"If he's still carrying the murder weapon," Quirk said.

"Jesus Christ," the mayor said. "You're going to search everyone in sight?"

"Everybody we seal inside the crime-scene area," Quirk said.

"Men and women?" the mayor said.

"While we're at it," Quirk said. "Why take a chance that the profilers are wrong."

"You'll have some female officers there."

"We will."

Even so," the mayor said, "the civil libertarians will go crazy."

"The civil libertarians got a better way to catch him," Quirk said, "I'm eager to hear it."

The meeting unspooled with reasonable efficiency, for a meeting. Mostly because nobody knew anything and it doesn't take very long to explain that.

At the end of the meeting, the mayor came over to my father and me as we stood to leave.

"Is this your daughter, Phil?"

"Sunny," my father said, "short for Sonya."

"The younger one," the mayor said.

"Yeah."

The mayor smiled at me and put out his hand.

"I remember you as a baby," he said. "I was running for city council from Hyde Park, your father used to drive me sometimes when he was off-duty. I understand you were on the job for a while."

"I was."

"And now you're helping the old man."

"I am," I said.

"That's great," the mayor said. "That's great."

We were in my father's small office at the new, spiffy
police headquarters when Quirk came in with a mildly
overweight man wearing flip-flops and one of those white
Mexican dress shirts that hang out. This one had vertical
black embroidery on the front. His hair was sand-colored
and curly. He wore oval-shaped glasses with black rims.

"Timothy DeVoe," Quirk said. "Phil Randall, and Sunny
Randall. They are working on the case."

We said how do you do. DeVoe's eyes, behind the black-
rimmed glasses, were red.

"Mr. DeVoe," Quirk said, "is Eugene Nevins's partner."

"I'm sorry for your loss, Mr. DeVoe," my father said.

"We both are," I said.

"Thank you," DeVoe said.

"Mr. DeVoe has confirmed the identification for us this morning," Quirk said.

"Are you okay to talk?" my father said.

"Yes," DeVoe said.

My father gestured him to a chair.

"When you've talked," Quirk said, "bring Mr. DeVoe back to my office and I'll have someone take him home."

My father nodded and Quirk left.

"Can you think of any reason why someone would kill your partner?" my father said.

DeVoe shook his head slowly and kept shaking it.

"He wore a wedding ring," I said. "Were you and he married?"

DeVoe held out his own left hand. He, too, was wearing a wedding ring.

"The day after the law passed," he said.

DeVoe's voice was shaky.

"Were you together long before that?" I said.

"We were together twenty-five years," he said.

"Anyone ever threaten either of you?" my father said.

"No. No one seemed to mind about the wedding thing."

"And no one threatened you or Mr. Nevins about anything else?"

"No. We were discreet, always. You know, we didn't kiss in public or hold hands on the street, that sort of thing."

I could see my father breathe a little deeper.

"Did you have any trouble, either of you, from anyone, for reasons other than your sexual orientation," my father said. "Any trouble. Any reason."

"Oh, no. God, no. We were very quiet."

My father nodded.

"Where did Mr. Nevins work?" my father said.

"I've told the other policemen all this already."

"I know," my father said. "I'm sorry. But it's one of the ways we do business, more than one of us asks you the same things."

"We run a small picture framing business on Boylston Street."

"In the Fenway area?"

"Yes," DeVoe said.

He gave us the address.

"Both of you worked there?" I said.

"Yes."

"Business do okay?"

"It was enough for the two of us," DeVoe said. "Our needs are . . . were simple."

"So no financial problems," my father said. "No big debts, not behind in rent or anything."

"No. We paid our bills and took a trip every Christmas . . . somewhere warm."

"Any enemies?" my father said.

"No, I told you, we were a very quiet couple."

And so it went on. As it had how many times before?

With how many sad people? All the same questions, mostly useless, but necessary to ask.

"Was there anyone else in Mr. Nevins's life?"

"He had a brother and sister."

"What are their names?"

And we'd talk to the brother and sister, and in-laws and nephews or nieces and friends and store customers, and we'd ask the same intrusive, tiresome, necessary questions that had so far in this case produced nothing. They were still being asked of those who knew the young black man who'd been the first in this second round. His name had been Theodore Eustis. He'd been a sophomore accounting major at BC.

"Friends?"

He gave us some names.

"Any other—I'm sorry, I have to ask—intimate relationships?"

DeVoe began to cry. As he cried he shook his head. My father waited. Slowly DeVoe got control.

"You think just because we're gay . . ." DeVoe said.

"I think nothing except I have to ask the questions," my father said. "I ask them of everybody."

He pushed a box of Kleenex across the desk. DeVoe took one and blotted his eyes and blew his nose. I pushed the wastebasket beside the desk around to where he could reach it.

"I know," DeVoe said. "I know you have to say what you say. I know that."

"How about other friends and acquaintances," my father said. "Could you give us a list of them?"

"I already told the other policemen I would do that," DeVoe said.

He was wearing down.

"I can't just rattle them all off. I'll go home, go through our addresses. I'll e-mail them to you."

"Okay," my father said. "Just give me the first, oh, five you can think of."

"God," DeVoe said. "I already did that, too."

"We don't vary much," my father said. "We all do the routine."

DeVoe took in a breath and let it out and listed three women and two men. My father wrote them down without comment.

"Why are we going through all this?" DeVoe said. "I know you're not being mean. But, damn, isn't it obvious that it's the Spare Change Killer?"

"We don't know it for a fact," my father said. "But even if we did. He's got to have a name. He's got to be somebody's acquaintance."

"Well, he's not one of ours," DeVoe said.

My father nodded.

"I know this is difficult, Mr. DeVoe," he said. "Do you have any employees at the frame shop?"

And so it went for another forty-five minutes, until De-Voe was drained dry and looked it. When I walked him back to Quirk's office, he was perfectly silent. When I said good-bye outside Quirk's office, he nodded silently. I left him slumped in an office chair, waiting for a ride home, and went back to my father.

"That was awful," I said.

"It always is," he said.

"And will be again," I said.

I t was a Sunday afternoon in my parents' backyard. I was drinking beer with my father. My sister, Elizabeth, had white wine, and my mother was drinking bourbon on the rocks. She always drank bourbon on the rocks. When my mother settled on something, she was slow to change.

"Do you think it'll work?" I said. "Sealing off the crime scene?"

"Won't do any harm," my father said.

Elizabeth had the same blond hair I did, though she was more aggressively blond than I was. We'd gotten our hair color from our mother, from whom Elizabeth had also gotten her taste in clothes. Today she was wearing big, round sunglasses and a pink dress with a low square neck and big puffy sleeves. She leaned forward and poured another glass of white wine.

"Don't you think this is a great wine?" she said.

No one commented that she was the only one drinking it.

"Spare Change doesn't seem dumb," I said. "If he is hanging around, won't he ditch the gun the minute he spots a search coming?"

"Probably, but we might catch him doing it, and even if we don't, we'll have a murder weapon. He might get flustered. Maybe we'll get a print."

"A man I'm seeing," Elizabeth said, "brought a case of this back from Napa Valley. He's a Harvard professor."

My father reached across the table and picked up Elizabeth's glass and took a sip. He swallowed and thought about it. He had on a short-sleeved maroon polo shirt, and his arms were still thick and muscular.

"Excellent," he said. "I'm not a wine drinker, but that's very good."

He gave the glass back to Elizabeth.

"It'll be a media circus," I said to my father. "Especially if we don't find anything."

"It's already a media circus," my father said. "It was a media circus twenty years ago."

"What are you two talking about," my mother said. "The two of you, thick as thieves."

"Just the usual," my father said, "cop stuff."

He got up and went to the cooler by the porch and got out a bottle of beer. He looked at me. I had half a bottle left. I shook my head. My mother watched him and then looked at me. She was wearing a bright blue pantsuit with a big sparkly flower embroidered on the front of the top.

"You should drink wine anyway," my mother said. "It's not ladylike, drinking beer."

"Maybe bourbon," I said.

"I trust bourbon," my mother said. She didn't pronounce the *r*. "I know just how much I can handle."

I nodded and sipped my beer from the bottle. In fact, I didn't like it all that much. But Daddy did.

"I prefer wine," Elizabeth said. "I'm reading a book about wine now. It's really interesting sometimes to try different ones."

Daddy came back with his beer and sat down.

"My friend, the Harvard professor, and I go sometimes to wine tastings," Elizabeth said. "We match the right wine with the right cheese, you know. It takes some learning, but the results are worth the trouble. My Harvard professor friend says he's going to get me a book on cheese."

"What is his name, dear?" my mother said.

"Charles," my sister said.

"Charles what, dear?" my mother said.

She rattled the ice in her empty glass and held the glass toward my father. He stood, took her glass, and went to get her another drink.

"Dr. Charles Strasser," Elizabeth said.

"Is he a Jew?"

"No," Elizabeth said. "He's German."

"From Germany?"

"No, I mean he's of German ancestry."

My father brought my mother her new drink. She took it and sipped some.

"A lot of Harvard people are Jews," my mother said.

"You assume he'll continue," I said to my father.

"No reason to think he won't."

"It's funny," I said. "I'm sort of rooting for him to keep on."

"I know," my father said.

"I don't want anyone else to die," I said. "But if he doesn't continue, we'll never catch him."

"Oh, blah, blah, blah," my mother said. "Why can't you ever talk about anything interesting?"

She was already starting to slur her *s*'s.

"It's not even something women should be talking about," she said. "Are you dating anyone?"

"Not at the moment," I said.

"And no wonder," my mother said. "Men like girls, not cops, for God's sake."

"I'm not actually a cop anymore, Mom," I said.

"Cop, shmop," my mother said. "You know what I mean. Who do you think you'll meet hanging around with cops."

"Maybe a man," I said. "Just like the man who married dear old Mom."

My mother didn't understand what I'd said. I could tell by the momentary flicker of fear in her eyes, before she hid it with bellicosity.

"And there's nobody going to want to marry a smarty pants, either," she said.

"I think Sunny was saying you married a cop and it hasn't been so bad," my father said.

"And if you'd listened to me, you could have been commissioner," she said.

My father smiled at her.

"Always been my problem, Em," my father said. "Too soon old, too late smart."

My mother offered him her empty glass. My father took it and went to get her another drink. I got up and went with him.

In the kitchen, I said to Daddy, "I thought she knew how much she could handle."

"She does," my father said, and smiled at me. "But she doesn't give a shit."

The next murder site was nearly perfect for the seal-off-and-search plan. The body of a young woman in a summer dress was found by a swan boat pedaler coming to work. It was facedown in three feet of water, bumping gently against one of the swan boats at the dock. On the dock, right by the edge, were a nickel, a dime, and a quarter. Several ducks were swimming about the dock curiously. The Public Garden was fenced and sealable. The only drawback was that at the beginning of a workday, it was full of people.

By the time my father and I arrived, there were cops at every gate and patrol cars slowly circling the Public Garden in case someone tried to climb the fence. Lines formed at each gate. Everyone protested that they'd be late to work. Cops don't care about stuff like that. These cops didn't, either. The lines got longer.

More cops, in uniform and plain clothes, were going over the park a foot at a time. The ducks had gone to one end of the swan-boat pond. The squirrels and pigeons trailed around near the cops, hoping that a peanut might appear. Reporters and photographers and TV cameras mingled with them. My father and I stood with Captain Quirk on the small bridge over the pond in the center of the garden. A woman approached us. She was tall and austere and reeked of Beacon Hill the way my father reeked of cop.

"Are you in charge," she said to Quirk.

"Of almost everything," Quirk said.

"I wish to register my strongest possible complaint."

"Except that," Quirk said, "I'm not in charge of complaints."

"I will not be patronized," she said. "This detention without due process is outrageous."

It was nearly noon. I knew that Quirk had been at the crime scene for a long time before we arrived.

"Young woman's death is pretty outrageous, too," Quirk said.

"Tragic," the woman said. "And you think detaining innocent citizens in the course of meeting their responsibilities is the way to solve it."

Quirk closed his eyes and stretched his neck for a moment. Then he opened his eyes and looked at her. Not many people could do the dead-eyed-cop look better than Martin Quirk.

"Lady," he said. "Fuck off."

The woman jumped as if she'd been poked. I put my hand on her arm.

I said, "Captain's had a long day, ma'am. Here, I'll walk with you over to this gate. Maybe we can squeeze you through a little quicker."

The woman had bright red spots on her cheekbones. Her breath seemed a little short. She came with me without speaking. The line wasn't any shorter, in fact, at this gate, onto Arlington Street. But, from my days on the job, I knew one of the cops checking people through. I winked at him and jerked my head at the woman. He nodded.

"Annie," he said to the female cop searching women. "This lady is next."

I turned the woman over to Annie. Someone in the line said, "Hey, how come she gets special treatment?"

The cop I knew looked at him and shot him with a forefinger. Then he began to pat down a black man at the front of the line. I went back to the bridge.

At ten minutes to one a sergeant named Belson, standing by a flower bed full of yellow tulips, put his fingers in his mouth and whistled to Quirk. Quirk nodded and walked over. My father and I went with him. In the bed, under some low leaves but not out of sight, was a black handgun.

"We got here quick enough," Quirk said. "He ditched it."

"So he was here," I said.

"If it's his," my father said.

"You want to bet we don't match it with the bullet in the girl?"

"No," my father said.

Quirk, Belson, my father, and I all looked slowly around the still-sealed-off park. Nobody said anything. Nothing presented itself. After a long moment, Quirk squatted on his haunches and studied the gun.

"Smith and Wesson," he said, "revolver . . ." He bent over to look at the barrel opening. "Thirty-eight."

He leaned forward onto his hands and straightened his legs and did a kind of pushup so he could smell the gun.

"Been fired recently."

He eased out of the pushup and got his feet under him and resumed his squat.

"But not in this flower patch," he said, "unless he bothered to clean up his brass."

"I'd look over there," Belson said, and nodded at the swan boat dock.

Quirk continued to sit on his haunches, looking at the flower bed.

"Stay with this, Frank," Quirk said. "I'll get some crime-scene techs over here, but I want you to be the only one touches the gun, okay?"

Belson nodded.

"You bag it, label it, take it to the lab, stay with it, wait for it."

"Okay, Marty," Belson said.

"Nobody but you and the lab guy touches it."

"Okay, Marty."

"I'll get some divers to look in the water for the shell casing," Quirk said.

"Three feet of water?" Belson said.

"Yeah, but you got to put your face in it. You want to do that without a dive mask?"

"Or with one," Belson said.

"I'll get some divers," Quirk said.

As we walked back toward the bridge, my father said, "He was here."

Quirk nodded.

"Maybe still is," Quirk said.

"Either way, we got his name," my father said.

"We got a name," Quirk said.

"You think he's walking around with fake ID?" my father said.

"I would," Quirk said, "I were him."

"Except for serial killing," my father said, "he may not be a criminal. He might not know how to get a fake ID."

I said, "There are websites, Daddy."

"On fake IDs?"

"Everything you ever wanted to know."

"I retired just in time," my father said.

"There must have been some people with no ID," I said. "What did you do with them?"

"An officer took them home or wherever so they could get one."

"Were there any for whom there was neither?"

"I don't know," Quirk said. "If they didn't have a home or

didn't have an ID anywhere, the instructions were to take them in."

"For not having ID?"

"Any charge the, ah, arresting officer could think of."

"My God," I said. "They'll be rioting in Harvard Yard."

On Thursday nights, Julie and I usually had supper together at the bar of the Metropolitan Club on Route 9
in Chestnut Hill. We were drinking blood-orange cos-
mopolitans, which were entirely exquisite. And so were we.
Julie was maybe a little more zaftig than I was, which I
didn't envy, though I think she thought I did. She had on
low-rider Cavalli jeans and a medallion-print white cotton
blazer over a black camisole. I was in my work clothes. Tan
faux-suede jeans, a yellow tee, and a blue cotton blazer. Both
of us had on open-toe heels. Mine were lower than Julie's.
But not repellently sensible.

"The bar scene here is always nice," I said to Julie.

"You think we should go somewhere else?" Julie said.

"That wasn't a criticism," I said.

"But how come a couple of hotties like us don't get hit on more?" Julie said.

"Maybe we don't invite it?" I said.

"I'm inviting as hard as I can," Julie said.

"It must be me," I said.

"You? You don't want to meet somebody?"

"I may have met more somebodies than I want to right now," I said.

"That policeman on the North Shore?" Julie said.

I shook my head.

"Oh," Julie said. "I'm sorry."

"It wasn't just him," I said. "He couldn't break with his ex-wife, but I couldn't let go of Richie."

"For God's sake," Julie said. "Richie's married to someone else."

"I know," I said.

"Do you ever see him?"

"Yes. We share Rosie, remember."

"Hell," Julie said. "Michael and I share children, for crissake. It doesn't mean I get moonie-goonie when I go to pick them up."

"It's not even that I have hopes," I said. "It's that what I have to share still seems to belong to him."

"What's your shrink say?"

"We're working on it," I said.

"What do you say?"

"Me?"

"Yes," Julie said. "Why can't you share yourself with someone else?"

"I love Richie," I said.

"Even though you divorced him?"

"Yes."

"That's crazy," Julie said.

"Is that a professional judgment?" I said. "Or just one pal to another?"

"Both. Love is an amalgam of pathology, rationalization, and fantasy. Men use it. They use it so they can jump your bones, and when they've done that enough, they use it so you'll take care of them."

"Care?"

Julie finished her drink and gestured to the bartender.

"You bet," Julie said. "Men are babies, in case you haven't noticed yet."

"Actually, I hadn't much," I said.

I knew this tirade. I'd heard it from my mother before I ever met Julie, and I heard it from her so often that I could almost lip-synch it with her. I also knew that after two drinks, when the faucet got turned on, there was no turning it off until the tirade had emptied out.

"They are. You have to tend to them sexually, see that their laundry is done, feed them, arrange their social life, make conversation for them, take care of their children, tell them all the time that they are a good boy."

"In so many words," I said.

"And if you don't do all of that, they go find another mommy," Julie said.

"You think that's what it's all about?" I said. "Oedipus?"

"Of course it is," Julie said. "They want to stay home with their mommy, and when they find out they can't, they start scurrying around looking for an adequate substitute."

Citing a concrete refutation of her generalizations was never effective when she was deep into her tirade mode. But I was bored, and the evening stretched long ahead, so I did it anyway.

"Richie wasn't like that," I said.

"You think," Julie said. "You're looking at him through those rosy romantic blue eyes. He's no different than all the rest."

"Gee," I said. "You know him better than I do."

"I do," Julie said.

She drank some of her fresh drink.

"I know them all," she said. "I see them clearly, without all that fuzzy claptrap you're peeking through."

"'Fuzzy claptrap,'" I said. "Wow!"

"You know what I'm talking about," Julie said. "That matrix of romanticism you apply to everything."

"You are on a really good run, Jule," I said. "'Matrix of romanticism.'"

"Laugh if you want to, but you know I'm right."

Julie drank some more of her blood-orange cosmo.

"Does your shrink believe in love?" she said.

"I think so," I said. "She has not called it 'fuzzy claptrap.'"

"Ask her sometime," Julie said, "what she thinks."

"I will," I said.

Julie looked up and down the bar.

"Two guys down at the corner of the bar are speculating about us," Julie said.

I nodded.

"I'm a little speculated out," I said. "So if something develops, you're on your own."

"Sure," Julie said.

She looked down the bar again.

"Gives me the choice of which one, then, doesn't it?" she said.

I nodded. I had finished my first drink, but the second one that Julie had ordered for me sat undrunk.

"Given how you feel about men and love," I said, "why do you want to choose either one?"

"That they're babies doesn't mean they're not amusing," Julie said.

"A minute ago you were telling me they were a waste of human resources," I said.

Julie grinned at me suddenly, and I remembered why we were pals.

"That was before I noticed them checking us out," Julie said.

"And now?" I said.

"Getting laid," Julie said, "is the best revenge."

I sat and drank coffee and ate doughnuts with my father in the front seat of his car in the parking lot of a Dunkin' Donuts shop in Union Square in Somerville. Rosie sat between us. My father was the only person I knew who had a car with room to seat three in front if one of them didn't mind the transmission hump. It reminded me of my childhood, when I would sometimes sit in front in the middle between my mother and father so I wouldn't fight with Elizabeth in the backseat.

"What kind of car is this?" I said.

"Crown Vic," my father said.

"I mean, who makes it?"

"Ford," my father said.

"Why'd we come over here for breakfast?" I said. "There's twenty Dunkin's closer to my place than this."

"I like this one," my father said.

He broke off a small piece of cinnamon doughnut and gave it to Rosie.

"It was the murder weapon," my father said. "All three murders."

Rosie chewed vigorously on her doughnut.

"But not the old ones, the ones you were on."

"No."

"So he was there, in the Public Garden, while we were?"

"Yep."

"So we have his name."

"Yep."

"Or a name."

My father gave Rosie another bite of doughnut.

"Daddy," I said. "She'll get fat as a pig."

He nodded.

"We going to start interviewing everyone we ID'd?" I said.

"Yes," my father said. "If we can find them."

"You think it's going to be a fake ID, too," I said.

"Yes."

"Maybe not," I said.

"No?"

"He hangs around to watch," I said. "Maybe he'd like the thrill of being investigated. How will we know who he is."

"We can narrow it some," my father said.

"With the FBI profile?"

"I'm not much impressed with those," my father said. "But most serial killers are white males. We could start by eliminating the females and the not-white men. See what happened."

"And there's probably some others you could eliminate," I said. "Very old, or in a wheelchair, or blind, whatever."

"So maybe we got a hundred real suspects," my father said. "Some of them will have alibis for at least one of the other killings."

"And some of them won't, and some of them won't even remember what they were doing three weeks ago."

"Still," my father said. "Say we're lucky. We might cut it in half, so we've got fifty suspects."

"One of whom is excited to be in the mix," I said.

"If he's in the mix," my father said.

"Unless he's stupider than he seems to be, powder residue won't be useful," I said. "Even if you don't wash, it's pretty much undetectable on your hands after about an hour."

"It can stay on your clothes for a while," my father said.

"Not if you wash them," I said.

"Which he probably did."

As we talked, Rosie fixed my father in a laser-like stare. Now, getting nothing for several minutes, she gave a piercing yap.

"Does that mean, 'Give me another doughnut, you dumb bastard'?" my father said.

"Yes," I said.

My father gave her another bite.

"Now shake your head firmly," I said. "And say, 'No more.'"

He did it. Rosie studied him for a minute and then turned around twice and lay down.

"I'll be damned," my father said.

"It's all in the early training," I said.

My father looked at me thoughtfully for a minute.

"Now you tell me," he said.

had taken off my makeup. I was barefoot, wearing sweats and a T-shirt. Rosie had just finished supper when Richie came to my loft, carrying a bottle of Irish whiskey. When Rosie saw him she did three spins and raced the length of the loft, turned, headed back, jumped on the bed, picked up her squeaky toy, jumped off the bed, dashed back to Richie, and squeaked her toy at him. Could I get changed and made up while Rosie was distracting him? No. He scooped her up with his free hand and held her while he sat at the small table in the bay and put the bottle of whiskey on the table.

"Uh-oh," I said.

Richie nodded. I looked at the bottle.

"At least it hasn't been opened yet," I said.

Rosie sniffed carefully at Richie's neck, seemed satisfied, and settled down in his lap, with her head hanging over his thigh.

"I need to talk," he said.

Don't you have a wife for that? I went to the kitchen and put some ice in a bucket, and brought it, with two lowball glasses, to the table. Richie poured us each a drink. I sat opposite him and picked up my glass.

"So," I said. "How 'bout them Sox."

Richie took a drink of whiskey. He was not generally much of a drinker, and on the occasions when he did drink, he didn't get drunk.

"I have your picture on top of a file cabinet in the back office at the tavern," Richie said.

"I hope I look better than I do now," I said. "You caught me unprepared."

"I've seen you more unprepared than this," Richie said.

"True," I said.

"And you always look good, prepared or unprepared."

I nodded. Richie looked like he always did, starched white shirt unbuttoned at the neck, the sleeves turned back over his forearms. Pressed jeans. Polished loafers. He rubbed Rosie's belly softly as he talked.

"Kathryn saw the picture a little while after we got married," he said, "and wanted to know why it was there. I told her I had forgotten to get rid of it, and would do so promptly."

I felt a little nip of something, maybe anxiety, in the bottom of my stomach. Richie sipped some more whiskey. I took a small swallow of mine to see what effect it would have on the little nip.

"But I didn't," Richie said.

"It's still there," I said.

"Yes."

"And Kathryn knows it?"

"Yes."

"Has it become an issue?" I said.

"A very large one," Richie said.

"So why don't you get rid of the picture?" I said.

The nip in my stomach had grown enough so I could tell that it was not anxiety as much as it was excitement. Richie finished his drink and put more ice in his glass and poured himself more whiskey. He looked at it for a moment, then drank some.

"I can't," he said.

"You can't."

"No."

"Did you tell her that?"

"Yes."

"That might have been unwise," I said.

Richie nodded. We were quiet. Rosie had shifted in Richie's lap so that he could rub more of her stomach. He and I looked at each other.

"It was true," Richie said.

"The truth is sometimes unwise," I said.

"Pretending doesn't work so well, either," Richie said.

I drank some whiskey.

"No," I said. "It doesn't."

Richie stopped rubbing Rosie's belly for a moment. Rosie shifted again so she could nudge at him with her nose. He nodded silently and resumed rubbing.

"What did she say," I asked.

"She said this was about a lot more than a picture."

"And she was right," I said.

"Yes."

"So how are you now?" I said.

"I'm sleeping in the guest room," Richie said.

"Are you talking?"

"No."

I tried to stay neutral. To ask honest questions. To help him. But I was having trouble with my focus.

"Don't you think you should?" I said.

"Yes."

"But?"

Richie shrugged.

"We're not talking," he said.

"You could have thrown it out," I said. "Or put it in a drawer."

Richie nodded. Still rubbing Rosie's belly with his one hand, he turned his whiskey glass slowly in front of him on the table with the other.

"I won't," he said.

I drank again. The whiskey had rounded some of the most jagged edges of my anxious excitement. But I still felt as if I wasn't getting enough oxygen. I got up and took my glass with me and walked the length of my loft. With her head hanging, Rosie opened her eyes and watched me upside down as I walked back. I didn't sit.

"You won't get rid of me," I said.

"I can't," Richie said.

"Welcome aboard," I said.

"You can't get rid of me," Richie said.

"No."

"That's what happened to you with that cop up in Paradise."

"Partly," I said.

"What was the other part?'

"He couldn't get rid of his ex-wife," I said. "Remember?"

Richie smiled with no visible pleasure, and shook his head.

"A goddamned daisy chain," he said.

I n response to some sort of internal clock, Rosie had jumped down from Richie's lap and gone to bed. On the table between us, the whiskey level in the bottle of Black Bush was a couple inches lower. It was dark outside my windows.

"How did we fuck this up so bad?" Richie said.

"Not easy," I said. "It took both of us."

"Let's establish something," Richie said. "Do you love me?"

"Yes."

"And I love you," Richie said.

"Yes."

"It's a place to start," Richie said.

"How about Kathryn?" I said.

"I was working on loving her," Richie said.

"Yes."

"But I couldn't get rid of the fucking picture," Richie said.

I nodded.

"My friend Julie says that love is just a collection of pathologies," I said.

"I like Julie," Richie said, "but she doesn't know anything."

I smiled.

"You know," I said. "That's true. I love Julie, but I never pay any attention to what she says."

"So why'd you quote her now," Richie said.

"To avoid saying things that matter more, I guess."

"We better talk about things that matter," Richie said.

"Yes," I said. "I can't be married."

"I sort of picked that up," Richie said.

"It's not because I don't love you," I said.

"I know," Richie said. "I didn't know it then. But now I do."

"I don't even know yet why I can't be married," I said. "I'm working on it. But so far I just know I can't."

"You couldn't when you married me the first time."

"No."

"Kind of sad," Richie said. "If we had been then who we are now, we probably wouldn't have gotten married."

I smiled.

"In which case maybe we'd have been able to stay together," I said.

"Could we call that irony?" Richie said.

"We could."

Each of us drank some whiskey.

"So what can you do?" Richie said.

"As opposed to not being able to marry?"

"Yeah."

"I do better with what I can't do," I said. "I really don't think I could live with anybody."

"Okay," Richie said.

"Okay?"

"We can love each other without living together."

I smiled.

"In fact, we are doing that now," I said.

"Sort of," Richie said.

"Sort of?" I said.

Richie nodded.

"Oh," I said. "That."

Richie nodded again. I drank a little whiskey.

"You're married," I said.

Richie nodded.

"I just broke off a very intense relationship," I said.

Richie nodded.

"I don't know what's right or even fair in all of this," I said. "But I know I can't be someone's mistress."

"I wouldn't want you to be," Richie said.

"You can't be married to Kathryn," I said, "and have me on the side."

"I know," Richie said.

"It's funny," I said. "We're both drinking, but we're not drunk."

"I know," Richie said.

"Or maybe we are so drunk we think we're sober," I said.

"We're not drunk," Richie said.

"What should we do?" I said.

"We could try sex, see how that works," Richie said.

"Not in the middle of confusion," I said.

Richie nodded.

"You're probably right," he said.

"We need to know just what it is we're doing," I said.

"Wouldn't that be a first," Richie said.

His hands were motionless on the tabletop. I put mine on top of them. We looked at each other without saying anything.

"It's a start," I said.

He nodded.

"We do love each other," I said. "There are worse places to begin."

"On the other hand," Richie said, "that's where we started the first time."

"Maybe we're smarter this time," I said.

"Hard to be dumber," Richie said.

"What was it that baseball player said?"

"Yogi Berra," Richie said. "It's never over till it's over."

I nodded. He stood. I stood and we walked to the door. On my bed, lying on her side with her feet sticking out and her head under my pillow, Rosie never stirred. At the door we kissed each other. More than friendly, less than passionate.

"We'll talk," Richie said.

I nodded. He opened the door.

"Don't throw the picture away," I said.

He smiled and went out.

My father and I sat in the homicide unit with Frank Belson at police HQ.

"We got the list boiled down to thirty-three," Belson said.

"Thirty-three suspects?" I said.

"Best thirty-three guesses," Belson said.

Belson had his jacket off and his tie loosened. His gun in its holster lay on his desk beside the phone.

"Anybody got a false ID?" my father said.

"Nope. They all check out."

"Anybody with a record?"

"Five of them," Belson said. "Two possession with intent, one unlicensed firearm, one assault on a police officer . . ."

"What was that?" my father said.

"Guy got into a fight in a bar, cruiser guys showed up, he took a swing at one of them."

"Did he by any chance happen to accidentally bang his head on something after his arrest?" my father said.

Belson smiled.

"Car roof, I believe," Belson said "His vision was a little blurred from the mace."

My father nodded.

"Anything else on him?"

"No," Belson said. "He had a fight with his girlfriend and tied one on. Girlfriend showed up in the morning with a lawyer and got him out. He's an orderly at City Hospital. Been there seven years. No other problems."

"How about number five," my father said.

"Smash-and-grab in a jewelry store," Belson said.

"Anything on the guy with the gun?"

"Lab's got it, but I'd say that it had never been fired."

"Why does he have it?" I said.

Belson grinned.

"You'll like this," he said. "Protection against the Spare Change Killer."

"Okay, so there's the five with records, what about the other twenty-eight?" my father said.

"FBI profile, age, no alibi, instinct, hope . . ."

"I wouldn't put too much on the age thing," my father said. "Could be a copycat. Could be twenty years old."

"We're not ignoring that," Belson said. "We're just trying to get some sort of probability list."

"And where do we come in?"

"We've invited all thirty-three in for reinterviewing," Belson said. "Thought maybe you could observe, see if anything hit you."

"You want us in the room or through the glass?" my father said.

"I'll leave that to you," Belson said.

"We'll take it case by case," my father said.

"Your call," Belson said.

"Anyone decline to come in?"

"Three people."

"Any reason?"

"They knew their rights," Belson said. "If we wanted them to come in, we'd have to arrest them."

"He might want to come in," I said.

"Same way he wanted to revisit the crime scene?" Belson said.

"Something like that."

"Might be," Belson said.

"When do we start?" my father said.

"Doors open tomorrow," Belson said. "Nine a.m."

My father and I sat in his car parked along the Charles River in Brighton and ate sub sandwiches for lunch.

"I saw Richie the other night," I said.

My father put his sandwich down on the dashboard and drank coffee from a big foam cup. He put the cup back in its holder and patted his lips with a paper napkin.

"Uh-huh."

"Daddy," I said. "Do you like Richie?"

"I did," he said.

"Do you still?"

"Don't think about him," my father said. "When you were with him, he was family. Now you're not, he's not."

"Do you think he's a good man?"

"If you do," he said.

"Besides me," I said. "Regardless of me."

"I'm your father," he said. "There's no such thing as regardless of you."

"Damn it, Daddy," I said, "I'm looking for advice."

My father ate some of his sandwich.

"About Richie?" he said.

"Yes."

"I don't know anything against him," my father said, "except that you divorced him."

"What if we got back together?" I said.

"You want that?" my father said.

"I don't know."

"Then I don't know, either," he said.

"What kind of advice is that?" I said.

"All I got," my father said. "I can't tell you who to love. I can't tell you if you ought to love him."

He stared through the car window at the river for a short time.

"But if you do love him," he said, "you need to act on it."

"He's remarried, you know."

"Doesn't matter. Married, single. You love him, you do what you need to do and you don't worry about anything else." He grinned at me. "Except, of course, your aging father."

"You feel that way about Mother?" I said.

"Yes."

"I didn't know you were such a romantic," I said.

"I know what a pain in the ass your mother can be. But I also know I love her."

"So you don't think it's crazy," I said. "Richie and me, again."

"I don't know if it's crazy, and I don't care," my father said. "You love him, you do what you need to do."

"What about his wife?"

"Not your problem," my father said. "He loves her, he'll stay with her. He loves you and he'll leave her."

"What do you suppose Mother would say about this?"

"Nothing you want to hear," my father said. "Or Elizabeth, either. I can deal with them."

"You can?" I said.

He smiled.

"Imagine them if I couldn't," he said.

"Julie says love is all just pathologies," I said.

"Julie's a dope," my father said. "You still seeing Dr. Silverman?"

"When I can."

"Ask her about it," he said.

"You act as if you know what she'd answer."

He shrugged.

"Ask her," he said.

"You know her?"

"Ask her that, too, if you care," my father said. "If it's in your best interest, she'll tell you."

"But you won't," I said.

"I never been shrunk," my father said. "But I know it's not

always a good idea for a patient to know a lot about the shrink."

"Yes," I said. "That's true."

We had both finished eating and were sitting, looking at the blank, gray river.

"So if I were with Richie, you'd like that?" I said.

"If you did," he said.

"What if I didn't?" I said.

"Then I wouldn't."

I laughed.

"You stubborn bastard," I said.

"But sensitive," my father said.

stood at the viewing window beside my father. There were chairs provided, but we both stood, drinking too much coffee, watching a parade of white males, ages forty to sixty, being questioned by detectives. Several of the men brought lawyers. But with or without counsel, the questioning was polite. No tough talk. No good cop/bad cop. No threats.

"Just need to go over a couple of things, sir. . . . Thanks for coming down, sir. . . . We're really grateful to you for your help on this, sir."

Belson stood with us, focused on the interviews, listening for every hesitation, watching for every eye shift. He reminded me of Dr. Silverman, who never missed anything said or gestured during our therapy sessions. My father was like that, too. He looked at the interviewees with such intensity that it was as if the force of his interest could pierce every façade.

Spare Change might be in there. Any one of these bland, middle-aged white men could have killed a large number of people for no good reason. Or at least no reason anyone understood.

"You lived in Minneapolis twenty years ago. . . . I know it's hard, but have you an address. . . . Is that in Minneapolis itself. . . . Suburban Minneapolis. . . . Were you employed during that time. . . . Do you have an address for that company. . . . No, no problem, we can find it. . . . Thank you for your time, sir."

And so it droned on. Belson and my father seemed oblivious to how boring it was. I was having trouble. *They're more used to it,* I thought. *They've been doing it longer.* Police work was a lot about listening to boring stuff that didn't do you any good. The trick was to stay with it, and listen to it, and spot the thing that mattered.

"I understand you're just doing your job. . . . Officer, I told another policeman already. . . . Twenty years ago? I don't know where I was twenty hours ago. . . . Yes, I already told another officer that. . . . I've never fired a gun in my life. . . . You don't think I had anything to do with these killings."

If anyone had said or enacted anything interesting, we could have discussed it and it would have helped pass the time. But no one did, so we stood and listened and watched as the time dragged past. I was sick of coffee, but there was no lunch in sight, and there was nothing else to do, and I felt like I needed a nap, so I drank some more.

Then at about ten past three, something interesting happened. A slim, balding man came in and sat down. What hair he had was cut very short. He wore an expensive-looking beige tee, tan slacks, and pale tan loafers with no socks. His watch was a Rolex. His slacks were carefully pressed. Everything he was wearing seemed new and fresh. When he came into the room, he walked to the interview officer with his hand out.

"Hi," he said. "Bob Johnson."

The cop didn't take his hand.

"Detective Bellino," the cop said. "Thanks for coming in."

"What's your first name, Detective," Johnson said. "I'm a first-name guy."

"Anthony," the cop said.

"How ya doing, Anthony," Johnson said.

My father looked at Belson. They both looked at me.

"Fine," Bellino said.

He slid a list of dates across the table to Johnson.

"Can you tell me, sir, where you were and what you were doing on those dates?"

"Hell, Anthony," Bob said. "My father is *sir.* I'm Bob."

"Sure thing, Bob. Where were you on these dates?"

Johnson picked up the list and studied it. He had crossed his legs, carefully hiking the pants leg so as not to spoil the crease.

"Wow," he said. "These are the Spare Change murder dates, aren't they?"

"Why do you think so?" Bellino said.

"Well, Anthony," Johnson said. "Isn't that what this is all about? The Spare Change Killer?"

"Can you remember where you were, Bob, on those dates," Bellino said.

"Oh God no, Tony. Do your friends call you Tony?"

"Tony is fine," Bellino said. "You can't remember what you were doing on any of these dates?"

"No, I'm sorry, but"—he shrugged—"tell you the truth, Tony, I am out and about almost every day. I'd really need to look at my book."

Bellino was looking at a notebook.

"It's a little surprising to me that you haven't," Bellino said. "We asked you the same thing before, and you gave pretty much the same answer. I'd have expected that you'd look it up by now."

"God, I know," he said. "Isn't it awful? You policemen are all working so hard to solve the case and we civilians . . ." He shook his head. "Of course I should have looked it up. But . . ." He shrugged and spread his hands.

"He's enjoying this," Belson said.

My father nodded.

"How you all doing with this case anyway?"

"Did you observe anything unusual in the Public Garden the day of the shooting?" Bellino said.

"Just a bunch of cops suddenly showing up," Bob said. "Too late, I guess."

Belson walked to the door of the interview room and opened it.

"Detective Bellino," he said. "We need you out here."

"Excuse me for a moment," Bellino said to Johnson.

"Sure thing, Tony. No rush."

Bellino came out. Belson closed the door. Inside the room, Johnson put his feet up on the table and crossed his ankles. He clasped his hands behind his head and leaned back a little in the straight chair.

"You interview him before?" Belson said.

Bellino looked at his notebook.

"No. Eddie Felice."

"What do we know about him," Belson said.

Bellino read from his notebook.

"Financial planner, self-employed. Works out of an office in his house. Told Eddie it's mostly house calls. You know, sit around the kitchen table in the client's house, tell him what stocks to buy."

"He trained in that?"

"Degree in finance from Taft. Some sort of financial-planner certificate."

"Married? Single?"

"Single," Bellino said.

"Ever married?" Belson said.

"I don't have it," Bellino said.

"Take a break," Belson said to Bellino. "We'll take him from here."

"I'll grab some lunch," Bellino said. "I been talking all day."

"Enjoy," Belson said.

Bellino went.

"He's having too good a time," my father said.

"I think I should talk with him," I said.

"Why you?" Belson said.

"He's a showoff," I said. "He'll show off more for me."

"Because you're a woman?" Belson said.

"Yes. Men show off for women."

Belson looked at my father.

"He strike any note with you, Phil?"

"Maybe," my father said. "He sounds a little like the letters."

"That ain't much, Phil."

"Didn't say it was."

"The killings are a kind of showing off," I said. "You know? *Look at me. See me. Look at this.* Let me see if I can get him to show off a little more."

In the interview room, Johnson was still leaning back, hands behind his head, casual. He seemed to be whistling softly to himself.

"Give her a shot at him, Frank," my father said. "She's awful smart."

"I've heard that," Belson said.

He walked to the door of the interview room, made a courtly sweep of his hand, and opened the door.

The room was fluorescent-lit and painted gray-green.
There was a white plastic-topped table and four matching straight chairs. Everything was pretty new and still sort
of clean. There were no windows except the one-way observation window. When I came in, Bob Johnson swung his feet
off the desk and stood. I could feel his stare. I was glad I
hadn't worn a skirt. I glanced at my reflection in the one-way
viewing glass. Yellow blazer, celadon tee. I looked good.

"Hi," he said, "Bob Johnson."

He put out his hand. I didn't take it.

"Sunny Randall," I said.

"The other cop wouldn't shake hands, either," Johnson said. "What's up with that, Sunny?"

"Cops get sort of used to not letting people get hold of them," I said. "Let's sit."

We did. Johnson looked at me carefully.

"Wow," he said. "Lady Blue."

I smiled. He smiled back.

"Or Lady Yellow, I suppose," he said. "Is that jacket real leather?"

"Let's talk about you," I said.

"You want to pat me down?" he said.

"That won't be necessary," I said.

"Damn," he said, and grinned at me.

"Could we run through it again," I said. "What brought you to the Public Garden at the time of the shooting?"

"I live in the Back Bay," he said, "Vendome Building, and three, four times a week I run down Commonwealth and around the Public Garden and back up. Keep that boyish figure."

"And you were jogging around the Public Garden at the time of the murder?" I said.

"Just after," he said. "I was cruising down Charles Street when I saw a bunch of cops rushing into the garden and so I banged a left and went in after them."

"Because?"

He grinned again.

"Curiosity killed the cat," he said. "I minded my business and kept jogging, I wouldn't be in here getting questioned."

I smiled back at him.

"I deserve it," he said.

I nodded.

"On the other hand, if I had just kept going, I'd never have met you."

"Did you see anything that might be useful to us?"

Johnson tilted his head back and stretched his neck and sat with his eyes closed. I waited. After a time he dropped his head back to its normal position and opened his eyes, smiled, and shook his head.

"Sorry, Sunny." He grinned. "Or Sunny, sorry. It works either way, doesn't it?"

"You saw nothing," I said.

Bob rubbed his chest absently, as if he were feeling his pectoral muscles and was happy with them.

"Not a thing," he said.

"You hung around to watch," I said.

I had nowhere to go particularly, but I wanted to keep him talking.

"Sure did," Johnson said. "Police stuff is fascinating."

"Why?" I said.

"Oh, you know. Movies, TV shows. Men"—he grinned—"and women, with guns."

"You like guns?" I said.

"For me? Personally? No. But I'm like everybody else. You know, cops and robbers? From the sidelines—fascinating."

I nodded.

"Sunny Randall," he said. "Great name."

"Thanks."

"You spell Sunny with an *o* or a *u*?"

"Have you been following the case, then?" I said.

He grinned again. He was certainly a grinner.

"'Yesterday my life was filled with pain' . . . remember the song?"

"Yes."

"Randall," he said. "Are you related to Phil Randall, the cop that worked on the first Spare Change killings? You know, twenty years ago?"

"Why do you ask?"

"Just curious, you know. I'm a curious guy." He laughed. "If I was a cat, I'd probably be dead."

"How would you know his name from twenty years ago?" I said.

"I read the papers. I told you I love law-and-order stuff. Said in the paper that he was coming back out of retirement to work on the case again."

"Are you especially interested in the Spare Change killings?"

"Are you?" he said.

"Yes," I said.

"Well, it's certainly an interesting one," Johnson said, "isn't it, Sunny."

"What's the most interesting part for you?" I said.

"Talking with you," he said. "You really are something to look at."

I thought of my father on the other side of the observation

glass. I had a momentary fear that he'd come into the room and take Johnson by the neck. But he didn't. I decided to try demure.

"Thank you," I said.

"You're welcome," he said. "You deserve it."

"Aside from me," I said, "why do you find the Spare Change case fascinating."

"Well." He leaned back and stretched his legs out in front of him and folded his arms. "He must be a fascinating guy. I mean, he goes about his business. He does what he does, on his own terms, without a word. There's no clues. There's no pattern. There's no motive. Nobody knows who he is. But everybody's thinking about him."

"Or her," I said.

He shook his head.

"No," he said.

"No?"

"No woman could do what this guy has done," Johnson said. "For more than twenty years? Never a slipup. Just walk up to somebody and pop!"

He pantomimed with his forefinger and thumb.

"No woman's going to do that," he said.

"You sound like you admire him," I said.

"Don't get me wrong. I condemn what he does. It's evil. But you gotta give the devil his due. He's good at it. He must be a pretty interesting guy."

"I wonder where he was for the last twenty years," I said.

"Between shootings?"

"Yes."

Johnson smiled.

"See what I mean. The man's inexplicable."

"So far," I said.

"You think you'll catch him?"

"Yes."

Johnson grinned at me.

"Attagirl," he said.

It's him," I said.

We were in Quirk's office.

Quirk looked at Belson.

"He was pretty odd," Belson said.

"Phil?" Quirk said.

"He was playing, Marty. You know how they get sometimes," my father said. "He was very coy."

"It was more than coy," I said. "It was masturbatory. He was exposing himself to me."

"You get people like that," my father said, "who sort of flirt with the crime. Doesn't mean they did it."

"He did it," I said.

"Maybe he wasn't flirting with the crime," Belson said. "Maybe he was flirting with you."

"He was flirting with me," I said. "But he was flirting with me about something covert and nasty. Like a dirty little boy showing me his pee pee."

"We need more than intuition," Quirk said.

"Thanks for not saying woman's intuition," I said.

"If I'd meant it, I'd have said it," Quirk answered. "Your intuition may be good. But we don't have enough evidence to disqualify him as police commissioner, let alone arrest him or search his place."

"We can pay special attention to him," Belson said.

"And we will," Quirk said. "We'll put a tail on him, twenty-four hours. And we'll see what kind of history we can get."

"Maybe when we get some," Belson said, "we'll talk to him again."

"If he's willing," my father said. "Unless we get some evidence, any cooperation from him is voluntary."

"He'll talk to me," I said.

"Voluntarily," my father said.

"Eagerly," I said.

"You're really convinced," Quirk said to me.

"Yes," I said. "Maybe in this case it is woman's intuition. You get to be a grown woman and you've been hit on by a lot of men."

Quirk grinned.

"You wanna leave the room, Phil?" he said.

My father shook his head.

"It's better than having daughters that don't get hit on," he said.

"Thank you, Daddy. . . . You get hit on enough, you develop a sense for when something icky is going on. This guy is icky. There's something sexual involved in his interest in the crimes. He gets a sexual charge out of talking about it. I go back to what I said before. He was like exposing himself to me."

"I've listened to the tape," Quirk said. "I think you did a nice job in there, Sunny, and I'm inclined to think you may be right."

"I am right," I said.

Quirk nodded.

"But if he's the guy," Quirk said, "and he's not gay, and there's a sexual thing going on, why isn't he just killing women?"

"I don't know," I said. "But there is a sexual thing going on."

"Well," Quirk said, "we'll have to find out what it is."

was at my Tuesday session with Dr. Silverman.

"I've got so much to talk about," I said.

Dr. Silverman smiled and nodded. I always felt sort of pale and insubstantial when I was with her. She was such a presence. Her black hair was so thick. Her eyes were so big. Her intelligence was so palpable.

"Two categories," I said. "Professional and personal."

Dr. Silverman nodded.

"I'm not sure where to start," I said.

"It doesn't matter," she said.

"Because we'll end up at the same place eventually," I said.

"Yes."

"I'm helping my father," I said. "On the Spare Change Killer."

Dr. Silverman nodded.

"Are you familiar with that case?"

"I am," Dr. Silverman said.

It was always amazing how pulled together she was.

"You know my father," I said.

Dr. Silverman made a little head movement that might have been a yes. Or might not have. I was free to go either way.

"He won't tell me how you know each other," I said. "He says that's up to you."

Again, the noncommittal nod. I took a breath.

"How do you know each other?" I said.

"We have a mutual acquaintance," she said.

I waited. She was quiet.

"That's all?" I said.

"These sessions are not about me, Sunny," she said.

It was the first time she had called me Sunny. I was thrilled.

"My father worked on the case twenty years ago, and in retirement is consulting on this one. I'm working with him."

"On the assumption that it's the same case," Dr. Silverman said.

"Yes. May I tell you about it?"

"Of course."

I told her about it, and about my long interview with Bob Johnson. She listened as she always did, with her full attention, leaning back a little in her chair. It didn't take very long. I was always amazed that things of such complexity and import seemed so easily compressed and de-emotionalized in her office.

"And you feel he is the Spare Change Killer?"

"I know he is."

"But you can't prove it."

"Yet," I said.

"We often know things in nondemonstrable ways," she said.

"But the courts require more," I said.

She smiled.

"Captain Quirk raised a question," I said. "Do you happen to know him, too?"

"I do," Dr. Silverman said.

"Mutual acquaintance?"

She nodded, I think.

"What was Captain Quirk's question?" she said.

"If there is something sexual in all this, why is the killing apparently gender-indiscriminate, and why is there no sexual molestation?"

"People are very good," she said, "at taking anything and shaping it into the symbol that their condition requires."

"You think that's going on here?"

"I have no way to know," she said.

"Talk to me a little about serial killers," I said.

Dr. Silverman was silent for a moment. She was older than I, but it would be difficult to say just how one would know that. She was positively beautiful. Her body was graceful and strong. Even in her self-abnegating shrink mode, she reeked of womanhood. The force of her self filled the room.

"There is a great deal of talk about serial killers," she said after a time. "And very little said. As I'm sure you know, they are predominantly white males. We can, and I'm sure you have profilers who have done this, offer a suggested outline of what they might be like. But the real issue, why they do what they do, is rarely clear."

"It seems as if it is often directly, or indirectly, sexual," I said.

"That might well be true of all human activity," Dr. Silverman said. "When we have a serial killer and can examine his life, we can find things that could explain him. But we could examine the lives of twenty similar people and find the same things, and they did not become serial killers."

"You're saying we don't know why serial killers are serial killers."

"To my knowledge," she said, "and I am not a specialist in serial killers, none has been discovered to have a unique emotional history."

"So Ted Bundy may have had a troubled youth," I said, "but so did a thousand other people that didn't turn out to be serial killers."

"Yes. It's why psychological predictions are very imprecise. Individuals react differently to the same stimulus. Psychological retrospection works much better."

"So what makes the difference?" I said. "Why did Ted Bundy become Ted Bundy?"

"Screw loose?" Dr. Silverman said.

"Don't get technical on me, Doctor," I said.

She smiled.

"Chemical imbalance?" she said. "Synaptic dysfunction? I don't know."

"You too," I said.

"And if you catch this Spare Change person, you still, quite likely, will not find out."

I nodded.

"How much can I trust my intuition?" I said.

She almost laughed. Good heavens. She had called me Sunny and now she'd nearly laughed.

"This is a morning for imponderables," she said. "Normally, intuition is the result of external stimuli interpreted by your own emotional condition. Neither, of course, is entirely reliable."

"Particularly the interior emotional condition," I said.

"True."

"If intuition is based entirely on emotion, it is probably useless."

She didn't comment.

"So is *intuition* just a fancy word for *guess*?" I said.

"I think we can pay attention to intuition," Dr. Silverman said. "As long as we are aware of its limits. A great deal in human behavior, after all, takes place below the level of rationality."

"Especially mine," I said.

She smiled and raised her eyebrows and cocked her head as if to invite more.

"I haven't even talked about Richie yet," I said.

She nodded.

"Are you familiar with Yogi Berra?" I said.

She smiled.

"It's never over till it's over?" she said.

"That's the one," I said.

Dr. Silverman went into the small ritual with which she ended every session. She glanced at the clock behind me, straightened slightly in her chair, and placed her fingertips together.

"We'll have to save Richie for next time," she said.

"And the time after that and the time after that," I said.

She stood. I stood. She walked to the door with me.

"And maybe the Spare Change Killer, too," I said.

"We have lots of time," Dr. Silverman said.

19

There is not really a way to force someone to give you an alibi, if the someone enjoys being a suspect. If we could establish an alibi for Bob Johnson for one or more of the Spare Change killings, then Bob's fun was over. If there was no alibi, then he'd remain a suspect. But we couldn't arrest him for not having an alibi, and the game would continue.

The police didn't have any evidence to get a search warrant. But I was not the police. I was a private investigator. I could do whatever the hell I wanted . . . sort of. Which was why, on a lovely late-summer Tuesday, I was about to break into Bob Johnson's condo with a professional burglar named Ghost Garrity.

Bob gave every evidence of going to an appointment. He had left five minutes ago, wearing a seersucker suit, carrying a briefcase, with a police tail behind him. Ghost and I stopped at the concierge desk. I gave the woman a card I had printed up the night before on my computer. The card said ZENITH SECURITY CONSULTANTS, with a downtown Boston address that didn't exist.

"Sonja Burke," I said. "My assistant, Mr. Garrity. The insurance company has asked us to look at security here. Nothing fancy. We just need to walk your corridors, look at exit flow."

The woman at the desk was a redhead wearing a nice green suit that set off her hair. She studied my card. Then she put it in the drawer of her desk.

"Sure, Ms. Burke," she said. "Help yourself."

"We'll start at the top and work down," I said. "We won't bother anyone."

The redhead gestured toward the elevators to her right, and Ghost and I got in.

"The apartment on the top floor?" he said.

"Next to the top, but if she's looking, I want her to see the elevator go to the top."

"Sure," Ghost said.

Ghost was carrying a big old briefcase. He had on a Palm Beach suit that was big for him, and wore one of the worst hairpieces I had seen in a while. It was a full shade of brunette darker than the graying hair that showed below it.

We got off on the top floor and walked the length of the

open corridor, which surrounded a central atrium, and down the back stairs to the floor below.

"How long to get us in there?" I said to Ghost.

He looked at the lock with scorn. He laughed as he opened his briefcase.

"I could open this thing with a Popsicle stick," he said. "But I don't need to."

He took a big ring of keys out of his briefcase and began to sort through them. I scanned the corridor so we wouldn't get caught.

"Open," Ghost said. "You need me anymore?"

"No," I said. "What are you going to tell the concierge?"

"I'm going out the cellar door," Ghost said.

"You cased the place?" I said.

Ghost grinned at me.

"I've robbed it before," he said.

I put my hand up, Ghost gave it a gentle high five, and he headed for the stairs. I didn't really like him leaving. I was a little uneasy about Johnson. But Ghost was a burglar, not a fighter. I had no right to ask him for protection. I went into Johnson's apartment.

It was a long apartment, but narrow, that looked out onto Commonwealth Ave. The blue walls were covered with art prints. The furniture was heavy masculine, with leather armchairs and thick-legged coffee tables. There was a kitchen, a den, a bedroom, and a bath. Everything was neat. The bed was made. All the surfaces were dust-free. The bath and kitchen were quite clean. To search the apartment thoroughly would take hours. I opted for the den. There was a couch and a desk. The desk was in front of the window. It was a dark wood, maybe stained cherry, with ornately carved legs and a green leather inlaid writing surface. There was a stand-up cordless phone on it, a planning calendar open to the current month, and an address book. I quickly looked up the dates of the current Spare Change killings in the planning calendar. There was nothing on any of those dates. The rest of the calendar was full of dates and notations, not all of them readable, but there was nothing on any of the killing dates.

The address book was a break. If he'd been a Rolodex man, it would have taken me forever. As it was, it took me only about five minutes to photograph the pages in the whole book with my macro closeup digital camera. I was an up-to-the-minute girl. The apartment reeked of silence. I could hear every appliance sound, the sound of the elevator, the sound of doors opening or closing, footsteps in the corridor. When I was done with my photography, I put the camera back in my purse. While my hand was in there, I rested it briefly on my gun. It was comforting.

I walked through the apartment, opened some closets, opened some drawers, found no guns, no clip file on the Spare Change Killer, no collection of incriminating letters, nothing to indicate that he wasn't clean, straight, orderly, and normal. Though maybe a little neat. In the bedroom, on the ornate bureau, was the picture of a young woman. It looked like a graduation picture. No inscription. No way to know who she was. I took a picture of the picture. Then I put the camera back and left the apartment. I heard the lock click behind me. I walked to the stairs. The concierge was supposed to think I'd been going floor to floor. I came out in the lobby, waved at the redhead, and went out. I was tense as I went out the front door. If Bob Johnson came back at that moment, I was busted. He didn't. I went out onto Commonwealth, turned right onto Dartmouth, and walked up toward Copley Place to get my car.

My father and I sat at the kitchen counter in my loft, looking at my computer. On the screen before us were the pictures of Bob Johnson's address book.

"So you just take the little whosis out of the camera," he said, "and stick it in the computer and it shows your pictures."

"Yes," I said.

"Can you print it out?" he said.

"Sure," I said.

I clicked on print.

"How do you know about all this stuff," my father said.

"I am a woman of the new millennium," I said.

The pages began to emerge from the printer.

"Of course," my father said.

He picked up the first page and began to look at the names.

"Any evidence we accumulate from using this list of names is inadmissible in court," my father said.

"If they know that the list of names led you to the evidence," I said.

My father nodded.

"Let's see what we find out, and then we'll let the DA worry about how we found it out," he said.

"We don't want to lose him," I said.

"If we can establish that it's him, not intuit but establish," my father said, "we won't lose him."

My father looked at the names on each sheet as the printouts emerged from the printer. At the end he shook his head.

"Nobody that I recognize," he said.

I brought up the photograph of the woman whose picture had been on Bob Johnson's bureau.

"How about her?" I said.

My father looked at the picture for a full minute. Then shook his head.

"Nope," he said. "I don't know her."

"That's a picture of her picture," I said. "The original is on the bureau in Johnson's bedroom."

"Any clues who it is?"

"No. I'd say she was twenty-one, twenty-two. The hairstyle is a little dated. It looks like a graduation picture to me," I said.

"There's no record of him being married," my father said.

"Lots of people have other kinds of connections," I said, "for which there would be no record."

"Ah, yes," my father said, "the new millennium."

"Anyone explored his years at Taft?" I said.

"Sure, and high school," my father said. "When his name first surfaced. Cohasset cops did the high school for us. Good academic record. No record of trouble. Not particularly active in whaddya call it, extra stuff."

"Extracurricular?" I said.

"Of course," my father said. "Didn't play sports, either, high school or college. He wasn't in a fraternity in college."

"Taft doesn't have fraternities anymore," I said.

"That would account for him not being in one," my father said. "The initial check was records mostly, nobody particularly remembered him."

"It's more than twenty years," I said.

"You have any sense of him from his apartment?"

"Mostly it was the absence of any sense of him," I said.

"Really?"

"Yes. The place was clean and orderly. There was food in the refrigerator, and shaving soap in the bathroom, that sort of thing. But no real sense of the man. Except for this photo, everything was art prints; trite, expensive furniture; matching drapes and bedspread."

"Like no one lived there?"

"No," I said. "Someone lives there, but it's like someone with very little personal self lives there. You know, no personality."

My father looked around the loft. Rosie was asleep on my bed. My easel stood under the skylight.

"Some people don't think much about where they live, some people do," he said. "We'll run down this list."

"It'll take a while," I said.

"Maybe we'll get lucky," my father said.

We were quiet, looking at the woman's picture on my computer screen.

"What bothers me most of all," my father said, "is that not one of the murder dates on his calendar is filled in."

"Nothing," I said. "All blank."

"But he had a lot of calendar notations," my father said.

"Yes."

"Big coincidence," my father said.

"Big."

Again we were quiet.

"How'd you get into Johnson's condo?" my father said after a while.

"A friend of Richie's," I said. "He had a key."

"How did he get a key?"

"Off a very large key ring," I said. "Which he carried in his briefcase."

"He have a name?"

"Gentleman named Ghost," I said.

My father stared at me for a moment.

"Ghost Garrity?" he said.

"Yes."

"Worse, and worse," my father said.

The cops spread out over the metropolitan area with the list of names I'd stolen. Boston cops, State cops, FBI, cops in Cambridge and Brookline, cops in Milton and Co- hasset, cops in any locale where there was an address in Bob Johnson's book. There were junior ADAs trying to match the names with any names they had collected in the back- ground check of the victims. Did any of the victims know any of the people in Johnson's address book? Did any of the people who knew the victims know anyone in Johnson's ad- dress book? There were FBI researchers working computers to cross-check against the first round of Spare Change vic- tims from twenty years ago. Serial-killer files were being read. Modi operandi were being compared. Ballistics technicians were trying to find a match between the Spare Change bullets and anything they had in the files. FBI profilers were studying data. Despite the massive effort, there wasn't much new data. So the profilers went over the old data again. Forensic shrinks were talking to everyone involved. They talked to me about my intuition.

"Do you know how many people confess falsely to high-profile crimes?" one of the shrinks said to me.

He was a thin, eager man with shaggy hair and a beard. His name was Tillman.

"I have some idea," I said.

"Mr. Johnson, if you are correct, is, in his way, perhaps confessing to you," Tillman said.

"Halfway," I said.

"That in itself would not, of course, mean that he is guilty," Tillman said. "Any more than the other, more outright confessions in this case."

"How many?"

Dr. Tillman shook his head.

"Several," he said.

"You're sure they are all fakes?" I said.

"One of them even brought the murder weapon."

"Really?"

"It was a cigarette lighter," Tillman said. "A replica Colt .45, like the cowboys used."

"Be a great red herring," I said. "Come in and confess in so foolish a way that you're dismissed as a whack job."

"Ms. Randall," Tillman said seriously, "you may trust me. This man was a whack job. So were several others."

"So is the Spare Change Killer," I said.

"And," Tillman said, as if I hadn't spoken, "your intuition, as you call it, may simply be wrong. The very existence of such a thing as intuition is somewhat uncertain."

"Call it an informed guess," I said, "if it makes you more comfortable."

"Informed by what?" Tillman said.

"By the subject's behavior and my experience."

"Both, of course, interpreted only by you," Tillman said. "It is a closed circle, don't you see. It has very little value in a forensic sense."

I wasn't supposed to be poaching in his field of speculation, and he was letting me know it.

"Neither do you," I said, and got up and left.

We were sitting on a bench near the crime scene in the Public Garden.

"Understand you were a little brusque with one Dr. Tillman," my father said.

"Pompous jerk," I said.

"Knows his stuff, though," my father said.

"So do I," I said.

"Good point," my father said, and handed me a file folder.

"Nothing much to report," he said. "Here's the bare facts we have on Johnson and the last victim."

All had returned to normal in the Public Garden. The

swan boats cruised slowly. The ducks followed them. People gave peanuts to the ducks. Pastoral.

I began to read the file. While I read, my father shelled and ate a bag of peanuts, paying no attention to the battalion of pigeons that swooped to our location when the first shell cracked.

The victim in the swan boat pond was a twenty-nine-year-old woman named Geraldine Robiski. She was a jewelry department manager at Filene's on Washington Street, and presumably was killed the night before she was found, while she was cutting through the Public Garden on her way home to an apartment on Newbury Street.

My father offered me a peanut. I shook my head.

The victim was single and lived alone. She'd worked at Filene's since she was in college and gone on, after graduation, to make a career in retailing, which, according to the people at the store, was going to be a successful one. She was attractive, dated often, but had no steady boyfriend that anyone knew about. Her purse had been found undisturbed on the swan boat dock. She had three credit cards, a driver's license, thirty-two dollars, some lip gloss, a couple of tissues, a comb, and some keys. The keys were for work, her apartment, and a 2001 Honda Civic parked in its space in the alley behind her building. According to the medical examiner, she was in good health, not a virgin, not pregnant, no sign that she'd ever been pregnant, no sign of sexually transmitted disease, nor any signs of physical abuse. She did not need glasses. Her teeth were good and showed signs of regular care. There was no alcohol in her. When she died she hadn't eaten supper yet.

Her dress came from Filene's, as did her undergarments. Her shoes were from a store on Newbury Street near where she lived. She had died of the gunshot, not from drowning. So she was dead, or nearly so, when she went into the water. Her parents had come on the train from Hamtramck, Michigan, to claim her body.

There was nothing about her that helped us. She was not noticeably like, nor noticeably unlike, the other victims.

Bob Johnson was forty years old, which made him old enough to have committed the earlier Spare Change murders. He had been born in Boston while his parents were still in school. His mother was nineteen, his father twenty. That had finished his mother's educational career, but his father, who was apparently something of a whiz kid, had gone on to earn three degrees and become a business professor at Taft. His mother had a boutique in Cohasset, where the family had moved when they could afford to, and where young Bob had spent most of his growing-up years. His grades throughout his school career were mostly B's. "Good student"—not a great one—was the report. Johnson went to Taft, where the tuition was probably right, and stayed in Boston. He'd worked several reasonably productive years at a big brokerage house before he'd gone out on his own at age thirty. He'd had no problems at the brokerage house that anyone could remember. According to the forensic accountants, his financial-planning business had flourished. His bank account was good. His investments were solid. He was single, had never married. There was nothing to suggest that he was gay. No one who knew him thought he was. He dated often but never the same woman for a long time. He owned his condo in the Vendome, on which he had a mortgage. He leased a 2003 Jaguar sedan. He was not otherwise in debt. His credit cards were paid off regularly. He had no problems with the IRS. He had not seen military service. A lot of people knew him, but none professed to be a close friend. On the other hand, no one had anything bad to say about him. He was not a member of any clubs. Not even a health club. As far as the cops could tell, he didn't golf, or fish, or play tennis, or lift weights. There was nothing to tell us what he did in his free time. I'd had several pedicures more exciting than Johnson's history.

I put the report down.

"If the victims had been bored to death," I said to my father, "this report would nail the case for us."

"Not an exciting guy," my father said.

"Unless my intuition is right," I said.

"Unless that," he said.

"Anyone talk to his parents?" I said.

"Both dead," my father said.

"Surprising," I said. "They were so young when he was born."

"Old man died early," my father said. "Mother last year."

A swan boat cruised by with its squadron of escorting ducks.

"Remember when you used to take me on those boats?" I said.

"Yes."

"I always loved that, especially if it was just me and not me and Elizabeth."

"Elizabeth says the same thing about you," my father said.

"We've always fought over you," I said. "Mother, too."

"I'm a prize all right," he said.

"We still do it," I said.

"If you say so."

"You don't see it?"

"Whether I see it or not," he said, "what you don't see is that all three of you have already won me."

"Daddy," I said, "you know perfectly well that for any of us to win, the other two have to lose."

He laughed, and put an arm around my shoulder.

He said, "Not going to happen, Pumpkin. Not going to happen."

Richie and I had dinner in Davio's next to Park Square. It was a big, handsome room and the food was good. Plus, Richie knew the owner, so we got a nice table. We ordered antipasto for two and a bottle of Sangiovese.

"You look great," Richie said.

"Thank you," I said. "You do, too."

It wasn't merely polite. We did look great. He was wearing what was almost a uniform for him: white open-collar shirt, dark jacket, lots of white collar and cuff showing. His neck was strong-looking. I was wearing a verdigris silk-and-spandex tank top, and a pleated cotton skirt in tan with verdigris at the hem. I carried the matching jacket, still proud of the shoulders. Richie liked skirts.

"Maybe," Richie said. "But you look better."

"Oh, okay," I said.

He smiled.

"You talk to Dr. Silverman about us?" Richie said.

"Not since these late-breaking developments," I said.

"But you will," he said.

"Of course."

"I'll be interested," Richie said.

I nodded.

"I'll share," I said. "Would you like to see someone?"

"I didn't grow up in a family," Richie said, "that values psychotherapy."

"But you seem to," I said.

"I'm different than the rest of my family."

We drank some wine.

"If you need to talk to someone, I can get a referral from Dr. Silverman," I said.

He nodded.

"I'm not ready yet," he said. "Though it doesn't mean I won't be."

I laughed.

"What?" he said.

"I'm imagining Uncle Felix," I said, "in therapy."

"There's a scary thought," Richie said.

"On the other hand," I said, "he and your father kept you out of the rackets."

Richie nodded.

"Mostly," he said.

"I don't want to hear about *mostly*," I said.

He smiled at me, and shook his head.

"I'm not in the rackets," he said.

"I know you're not," I said.

"My father and Uncle Felix," Richie said. "They kept me out. Felix was sort of in charge of that. He taught me to fight. He taught me to shoot. He taught me how to run a mob, in case I had to. Then they sent me to college. And I had to account to Felix for my performance."

"I remember," I said.

"They're a little tough on other people," Richie said. "But they take care of their own."

"I know," I said. "What do you suppose Felix would say if you told him you were seeing a shrink?"

Richie twirled his glass of red wine slowly by the stem while he thought about that.

"'Whatever you need to do, Richard,'" he said in a fair copy of Felix's cavernous rasp. "'You got problems the shrink can't solve, you come see me.'"

We ate a little. We drank a little wine. The sommelier came by and spoke to us, and picked up the bottle, and refreshed our glasses, and strolled on.

"I've moved out of the house," Richie said.

I nodded.

"I'm staying at the Phillips Club on Avery Street," he said.

"How's Kathryn?" I said.

"Not good."

"What does she understand this to mean?" I said.

"I don't think she knows yet what she understands," Richie said.

I nodded again.

"What do you understand this to mean?" I said.

Richie twirled his glass some more, watching the dark surface of the wine. Then he raised his eyes and looked directly into mine. It was almost as if I were being penetrated.

"I'm going for it all?" he said.

I was conscious that my breathing had become shallow and quick. My throat felt tight. Around me the restaurant continued in real time. People were dining and drinking and chatting and being pleased and being annoyed. Time had slowed at my table. Everything had receded a little. We were alone in a slightly different time and place. Living at a slightly different speed. I swallowed some wine so that my voice would work.

"What's *all*?" I said.

"You," he said.

"It's a pretty big gamble," I said. "I don't know exactly if I can be the one you think I am, or want me to be."

"You love me?" he said.

"Yes."

"You know that."

"Yes."

"Then I'm going for it," he said. "I gave it up too easily last time."

"God," I said. "I'm scared to death."

"Me too," he said.

The first letter came on a Saturday morning while I was thinking about the weekend. I didn't have a date. And, in truth, I didn't want one. Sunday, I thought I might sleep as late as Rosie would let me, and make myself a big breakfast and wash my hair, maybe manicure my nails, maybe rearrange my closet. I might paint some, too, when the sunshine through my skylight was right.

The mail came around eleven-thirty. As soon as I saw the block printing on the address, I knew who'd sent it. I opened it carefully. The letter inside was block-printed as well. Plain white paper. Plain black felt-tip pen. All it said was: "Hi, Sunny, welcome aboard."

I read the message twice, then folded the letter carefully and put it carefully back in its envelope. I went to my desk, which I never sat at, at the far end of the loft, next to the bathroom, and got an 8½-by-11 manila envelope and put the letter in its own envelope in there and fastened the little metal clasp. I put the envelope on the small table in the bay, where I usually ate if there was company.

I went to the door. It was locked. I went to my bedside table and took my gun out and put it on the kitchen counter, where I usually ate when I was alone. There were new issues of *Vogue* and *Vanity Fair,* the half-read newspaper, and the rest of the mail. I sat back down, poured some more coffee, shuffled the mail around, got rid of the junk, and put the bills in a neat stack beside the toaster. Then I looked over at the manila envelope on the table.

"Bob Johnson," I said out loud, "you son of a bitch."

Rosie pricked her ears and looked at me carefully to see if "Bob Johnson, you son of a bitch" had anything to do with me giving her a dog biscuit. I got off the counter stool and walked to the windows and looked down at the street. My loft was on the fourth floor of a converted warehouse in South Boston, near Fort Point. The street looked like it always did. Cars parked on both sides. Some traffic on a Saturday morning. No Bob Johnson. Nothing that didn't belong.

There had been a father/daughter sidebar piece to the ongoing Spare Change Killer coverage in the paper. The story mentioned my father and me by name. And I'd been mentioned in several instances by people reporting the story on television. The fact that he sent me the note after I'd interviewed him at police headquarters proved nothing. I walked back toward the kitchen.

I looked at my gun on the counter. It was comforting to have it there. On the one hand, there was no special reason to think he'd attack me. He had never done that. He'd written to my father for several years in phase one of the killings, and had never made any attempt to harm him. On the other hand, I was not my father, who was sort of like a pleasant Cape buffalo. . . . I didn't look dangerous. . . . I was a woman, and a young woman at that . . . attractive in my own humble way . . . and I had felt his flirtation in the interview room. . . . He'd been excited in the interview room.

"About what?" I said to Rosie.

She looked hopeful again. I looked down at her and shook my head. Rosie let her ears flatten and turned away. She went to the bed and jumped up and lay with her head on her paws, looking at me disgustedly.

I walked back to the window. . . . His excitement had been sexual. . . . There was something sexual in him and in the whole case . . . but there was nothing sexual about the crimes . . . no rape . . . nothing. . . . I went to the phone and called my father.

was having brunch with my family at my mother's favorite place, an inn west of Boston, notable for its commitment to chintz curtains. My mother considered the place to be as cute as a bug's ear. My sister seemed to think the food was good. My father registered no opinion but ate very modestly. At the buffet table, I'd ordered scrambled eggs, and the server, in her mop hat, had sliced them off a loaf.

"Lab got nothing off the letter," my father said to me.

"I didn't think they would," I said.

My father had a lot of fruit on his plate and one sausage. He and my sister each had a Bloody Mary. I had tomato juice. My mother had bourbon on the rocks. It probably wasn't, I thought, because she liked it best. It was what she knew how to order, and she feared change.

"Sunny," my mother said, "aren't you going to finish your eggs? There's a lot of good protein going to waste there."

"I'm saving the best for last," I said.

"I don't much like him writing you," my father said.

"Who?" my mother said.

"He wrote you," I said to my father.

"Who wrote who?" my sister said.

"I'm not my daughter," he said.

"What on earth are you two talking about?" my mother said.

"Just the case, Em. The Spare Change thing."

"Oh, pooh to the case. We're having brunch, the least you two could do is talk about something the whole family can talk about."

"Sure," my father said. "We'll revisit this later, Sunny."

"It'll be fine," I said. "What have you been up to lately, Mother?"

"Well," she said. "You know how frantic everything is around Christmastime, so Millie Harrison and I have found a place where you can buy Christmas stuff anytime. We went over there yesterday and got Christmas cards, enough for everybody on the list, and tree ornaments, and some fabulous new kind of candles for the window. They have batteries so you don't have to have all those ugly cords showing."

"Fab," I said.

My father had a bite of his sausage. His face remained impassive, but I saw him move the rest of the sausage to the far edge of his plate with his fork. The waitress came by and brought my mother another bourbon. My mother looked pleased.

"We would have gone over on a weekday," my mother said. "Any smart shopper knows it's always more crowded on a Saturday. And I like to think I'm a pretty smart shopper."

"That's for sure, Em," my father said.

"But, you know," my mother said, "we are having a big round-robin bridge tournament, and it was at my house on Thursday, four tables of bridge, so I had to get ready for that. Hors d'oeuvres, a dessert. I got a bunch of those little frozen hors d'oeuvres, little hot dogs in pastry dough, and those little meatballs, and I put out a big bowl of nuts and bolts. Everybody told me it was better than any restaurant."

"I'll bet it was," I said.

With his fork, my father speared a chunk of pineapple and ate it.

"And," my mother said, "when we played, I was with Gladys Greer, and we won at our table and are going to the next round Thursday at Polly's house."

"Congratulations," I said.

"You know your bridge, Em," my father said.

"I have something that might be of interest," Elizabeth said.

She looked like me, except on a slightly larger scale. Elizabeth liked being larger. She was always wearing tight tops and sticking her boobs out. On the other hand, I was a full size smaller. I was never sure whether I envied her or she envied me. Probably both.

"What's that, honey?" my father said.

"I think I'm getting married."

"The Jew?" my mother said.

"He's not Jewish, Mother. It's a German name."

"Are you pregnant?" my mother said.

"Mother!"

"I call a spade a spade," my mother said. "If you're pregnant, the marriage has to be fast."

"I'm not pregnant," Elizabeth said.

"He give you a ring?"

"Not yet."

"You better make sure he gives you a ring," my mother said.

"We love each other," Elizabeth said. "I think that's quite enough."

"Love goes right out the window," my mother said, "if there's no money."

My father smiled at Elizabeth.

He said, "Lucky I held on to my job, huh?"

"You can joke all you want, Phil," my mother said. "But you know I'm right."

My father reached over and patted her hand.

"Almost always, Em," he said. "Almost always."

"Congratulations," I said to my sister.

She nodded.

"It'll be a fall wedding," she said. "I hope you'll be the matron of honor, Sunny."

"I'd be thrilled," I said.

"Maybe we can have the reception here," my mother said.

They began to discuss the pros and cons of a wedding reception here in Chintz City. I drank my tomato juice and wished it were stronger.

26

We were walking Rosie down near the Design Center. "I went to Vietnam out of there," my father said.

"The Design Center?"

"Used to be the South Boston Army base," my father said. "I took my physical there."

"It would make you smile now," I said, "if you went in there."

Rosie stopped to investigate a beer can in the gutter.

"Lets talk about the letter from Spare Change," my father said.

"I don't think it's worrisome," I said. "I think it's just part of his flirtation. He wrote you, now he's writing me. I bet he smirks while he writes it."

Rosie satisfied herself that the beer can was irrelevant, and we moved on.

"You might want to remember that this guy may have killed a dozen people."

"But never anyone investigating him."

"He's never been investigated by a good-looking woman," my father said. "If there is a sexual angle to these killings, like you say there is, your presence changes things."

"Yes," I said. "I've thought about that."

Rosie stopped again. There was a seagull standing on the sidewalk ahead of us. Rosie stared at it. Was it danger? Was it edible? Was its edibleness commensurate with its dangerousness? I could almost hear her little brain meshing. My father reached down and picked up some gravel and threw it at the seagull. It flew up and away. Rosie watched it, then turned her head to stare at my father. He shrugged at her.

"Serve and protect," he said to Rosie.

She wagged her tail and we moved on.

"Would you consider getting off the case?" my father said.

"Daddy," I said. "This is what I do."

"I know, that's why I'm asking, not telling."

"I'll stick, Daddy. I have a gun. I can shoot. I used to be a cop. Now I am a private detective. What am I if I go home and hide any time there might be danger."

My father nodded.

"I love Em," he said. "And I love Elizabeth. As much as I love you."

"I know," I said.

"But you're the one I can talk to," he said. "I'd miss that."

"I'll be careful," I said. "And remember, I'm pretty good. You know who taught me."

He smiled.

"Good point," he said.

A man coming from the Design Center paused as he passed us and looked at Rosie. He had his cell phone out but hadn't dialed.

"Is that a purebred?" he said.

"Yes."

"What is she?" he said.

"A miniature English bull terrier."

"Wow," he said. "Are they supposed to have no forehead like that?"

My tone was as icy as I could make it.

"She's an outstanding representative of the breed," I said.

"I'm sure," the man said, and walked on, dialing his cell phone.

"Dolt," I said.

My father seemed amused. Past the Design Center, we turned and started back toward my loft.

"What do you think of the man Elizabeth is going to marry?" I said. "I haven't met him."

"She loves him, I love him," my father said.

"Yeah, yeah," I said. "But if you knew him without any involvement of Elizabeth, what would you think?"

"I'd think he was a self-absorbed Brattle Street jerkoff," my father said.

I smiled.

"Come on, Daddy, tell me what you really think."

"Too much education," my father said, "too little experience. Knows everything about nothing."

"Elizabeth has not always loved either wisely or well," I said.

"She thinks she needs a man to be whole," my father said.

I stared at him.

"She does," I said. "You think about stuff like that?"

My father smiled at me.

"Only when I'm with you," he said.

It was a woman again. Near Jamaica Pond. The cops did their dragnet as quickly as they could, but the Jamaica way is much more uncontained than the Public Garden, and they dragnetted substantially fewer people. Bob Johnson wasn't one of them.

"Two women in a row," I said. "Does that mean anything to any of us?"

"He's done that before," Quirk said. "He's done three men in a row. I wouldn't put too much weight on it."

"Coins?" I said.

"The usual," Quirk said. "Three, on the grass beside her head."

We were in his office with my father and Frank Belson.

"What kind of weapon?" my father said.

"Thirty-eight," Quirk said. "No cartridge casings at the scene."

"Do you know where Bob Johnson was during the time of the shooting," I said.

"No," Quirk said.

"Don't you have a tail on him?" I said.

"He shakes it whenever he feels like it," Quirk said. "Which is often. He shook it the night of this murder."

"How many men?" my father said.

"One."

"No wonder," my father said.

Quirk nodded.

"I know as well as you do that it takes at least four to do a decent surveillance," he said. "Four men times three shifts is twelve men. I don't have twelve men."

"Even for this case?" I said.

Quirk shook his head again.

"Not for a guy against whom we do not have a single scrap of evidence," Quirk said.

"He's the one," I said.

"You know that," Quirk said. "But nobody else knows it. There's other police work being done in the city. The best I can do is one man per shift. I'm lucky to get that. It's a testimony to my respect for you, Sunny."

"And he knows he's being tailed," my father said.

"Sure," Quirk said. "He likes it. It's fun for him. Hide-and-seek."

"And you lose contact with him regularly?" I said.

"Most days."

"Smart," I said.

"Yeah," Quirk said. "We were out of contact during the time of this murder, but we were out of contact twenty other times, when there was no murder."

"If it's him," Belson said.

"And you can't requisition more surveillance," my father said.

Quirk shook his head and continued to shake it as he spoke.

He said, "You haven't been retired that long, Phil."

My father nodded.

"Yeah," he said. He mimicked an official voice. "'Excuse me, Commissioner, but one of the women working on the case has an intuition that it's Johnson.'"

"And maybe, a little bit, yours and mine," Quirk said.

"Mine too," Belson said. "But we may be wrong."

"So why does he keep shaking the tail?" I said.

"Fun," Belson said. "Same reason he was so lively when we brought him in to interview. He may be a freak. He may be getting his rocks off being suspected of a crime. He may be excited playing cops and robbers. Doesn't mean he did it."

"Case like this brings out a lot of whack jobs," my father said.

"He's the one," I said.

"We don't have one other goddamned thing on him,

Sunny," Quirk said. "So even if I think you're right, there's nothing I can do about it."

"There may even be a copycat at work," Belson said. "For all we know, more than one."

We were quiet. "Maybe I should talk to him," I said.

"No," my father said.

"Daddy, we've already had this argument and I won it," I said. "He's no more dangerous to me than he would be to any of you."

"I want to be there," my father said.

"No," I said. "I'm what winds his watch. You being there would be counterproductive. Any of you."

"If she's right and he's the one," Quirk said, "she's also right about this. She needs to see him alone."

"In a public place," my father said.

"I don't want him to kill me, Daddy. I'll meet him at Spike's."

"Spike?" Quirk said.

"Sunny's pal. Runs a restaurant. Claims he's the world's toughest queer."

"Is he right?" Quirk said.

"I think so," my father said.

"Good choice," Quirk said. "We could wire you."

"No," I said. "He'll expect that."

"You're pretty sure about this guy," Belson said.

"I am," I said.

"You're sure he'll meet you?" Belson said.

"Absolutely," I said.

"Do not," my father said slowly, "be alone with him."

"I won't," I said.

"And make sure Spike is in the room when you sit with this guy."

"Yes, sir," I said.

"I know how you are," my father said. "I shouldn't have brought you in on this."

I smiled at him, sitting beside me, and patted his forearm.

"Too late," I said.

I met Julie at workday's end, for a drink at Noir in the Charles Hotel, which was only a couple of blocks from the little office where she did counseling. Julie had a glass of chardonnay. I had a sauvignon blanc.

"Originally I sort of knew him because I had his wife in therapy," Julie said. "Then I met them one day, in the Chestnut Hill Mall, outside Bloomie's, and she introduced me to him, and there it was, you know, 'the heavenly jingle when two tingles intermingle'?"

"Your patient's husband?" I said.

"You play it as it lays," Julie said. "He called me a couple of days later and invited me to lunch."

"And you went."

"Sure. You feel that buzz, you don't let it pass. Besides, knowing him, I might be able to help her."

"By fucking her husband?" I said.

Julie laughed.

"Don't be coarse," Julie said.

"I'm not the one being coarse," I said.

"And why are you so sure we're having sex?"

"Crazy guess," I said.

Julie laughed.

"You know me so well," she said.

"I do," I said. "But poaching a patient's husband may be a new low."

"It may really be good for our therapy," Julie said. "And she'll never know."

I nodded and didn't say anything. I was pretty sure Dr. Silverman would question Julie's therapeutic analysis. I was also pretty sure that Julie wasn't motivated by the therapeutic considerations.

"And . . ." Julie paused and drank some wine. "He might be the one."

"The one?"

"The one," she said. "I mean, when we're together . . . it's electric. When we make love . . . I think sometimes I'm going to faint . . . honest to God. My head swims."

"So you don't think love is an amalgam of pathology, rationalization, and fantasy?" I said.

"A rose by any other name," Julie said.

"Really?" I said.

"This might be the real thing," she said.

I thought that she'd probably had the real thing with Michael, but was nowhere near ready for it. She hadn't become more ready since their divorce.

"What does he say about his wife?" I asked.

"She's a decent woman, he says. Okay mother. But she's inhibited, and he finds her kind of boring."

"Sexually inhibited," I said.

"Yes," Julie said.

She sounded startled by my question, as if there were no other kind of inhibition.

"And you're not," I said.

Julie laughed and drank some wine.

"You want details?" she said.

"No."

When Spike still thought he might have a career in show business, and had two suits for partners at his restaurant, they called the place something cute that I can't even remember now. When Spike retired from show business (or vice versa), he bought out the two partners, and the place was now named Spike's. It was probably a bar that served food more than a restaurant, but Spike always called it a restaurant.

By design Spike was behind the bar when I met Bob Johnson there. I was in a flossy version of my basic outfit: designer jeans, a white T-shirt, a dark jacket, and a matching shoulder bag with a gun in it. Bob came in, wearing a blue-flowered sport shirt and a Panama planter's hat.

"Sunny Randall," Bob said. "This is a treat."

"Thanks for coming," I said.

"Oh, no," he said, "my pleasure."

"Will you have a drink?"

"Splendid idea," he said.

Spike came around the bar and walked to the table. He weighed maybe 265, and there was very little shape to it, and not much definition. That was illusory. I had seen him in action. He was as strong as a grizzly bear, with the same quickness and ferocity.

"My waitstaff is a little busy," he said. "May I get you folks something?"

The waitstaff had been warned not to recognize me, but I knew that Spike wanted a closeup of Bob. Bob ordered a Tanqueray and tonic. I had a glass of sauvignon blanc.

"So is it this case you're working on?" Bob said after Spike went to get the drinks. "Or is it my irresistible self?"

"Hard to say," I answered. "Some of both, I suppose. It just felt, when we talked at the police station, that there was a connection."

"My God," he said. "I felt that, too."

Spike came back with the drinks.

"Enjoy," he said.

He went back behind the bar and appeared to pay us no further heed.

"Huge man," Bob said.

I nodded.

"I wonder if it's fat or muscle," he said.

I shrugged.

"He the regular bartender?" Bob said.

"I think he's the owner," I said.

Bob nodded.

"Filling in," Bob said.

He sipped his drink.

"Good stuff," he said. "You come in here much?"

"Now and then," I said. "It's kind of convenient to where I live."

He nodded and looked around the room. There was a bowl of peanuts on the table, and he took a small handful and popped one peanut into his mouth.

"Doing a nice business," he said.

I was determined to let him lead the conversation, and I was prepared to make small talk with him until he did.

"Yes," I said. "It's nearly always busy when I'm here."

"Do you know the owner?" he said.

"Not really," I said. "I've seen him in here. But I don't know him in any meaningful sense."

Bob looked at Spike for a while. Spike bothered him. He had very good instincts. He was like a dog sniffing around a new place. He ate a few peanuts. After a while he shifted his look to me.

"So," he said, "Sunny, you want to talk with me about the case?"

"Sure," I said.

"Well," he said. "I think first you have to accept the fact that this guy is no ordinary criminal."

"I know," I said. "I know."

He smiled.

"Got you buffaloed, hasn't it," he said.

I nodded.

He leaned back a little and stretched his legs out to the side. He was wearing white slacks and a pair of sandals. He'd obviously had a pedicure. He turned his glass for a moment on the tabletop, then picked it up and finished the drink. When he put the glass down, Spike, also by prearrangement, walked from the bar.

"May I get you another?" Spike said.

"Be a fool to say no," Bob answered.

Spike went back to the bar and started on Bob's second drink. If Bob got a little drunk, it couldn't hurt.

"Got everybody buffaloed, hasn't he," Bob said. "Your father, everybody."

"He certainly has," I said.

Spike came back with Bob's drink, set it down in front of Bob, and went back to the bar.

"Our problem," I said, "among many, is that we can't figure out a motive or even a pattern."

"Doesn't mean there isn't one," Bob said.

"A motive, or a pattern?" I said.

"Both," Bob said. "Nothing sane happens without motive or pattern."

"And you think this guy is sane?" I said.

"Of course," he said.

"How could somebody like the Spare Change Killer be sane?"

Bob smiled.

"Because you don't understand the crimes, you decide they are insane," Bob said. "Was Bundy insane? Or Richard Speck? If they were, how could they be guilty?"

"But why would somebody want to go kill a bunch of people he doesn't even know?"

"Why indeed?" Bob said. "That would be the question, wouldn't it."

The space between us was thick with sexual tension. There was something voyeuristic going on, as if we were talking in a sexual code that I couldn't translate.

"You have any theories?" I said.

"Hell, Sunny," Bob said. "I'm full of theories. How 'bout you? You're the detective."

"I'm interested in yours," I said. "You seem such a perceptive man."

His sexual excitement hadn't waned. It hovered like incense between us. He smiled modestly.

"Well, this true-crime stuff fascinates me," he said. "I suppose if I weren't so nosy, I wouldn't have gotten rounded up in the Public Garden that day."

"Curiosity is natural," I said.

"That's right," he said. "And if I hadn't been nosy, we wouldn't be sitting here now."

He picked up another small handful of peanuts and shook

them loosely in his hand, the way you might shake dice, before he ate one. He drank some of his gin and tonic.

"So," he said. "Theories."

"Theories," I said.

"Maybe he does it because he likes it."

"Killing strangers?"

"Maybe it makes him feel good," Bob said.

"Exercising that kind of power?" I said.

"Could be," Bob said.

He was much less relaxed now. His posture was unchanged, but there was a rigidity to it that was not comfortable.

"Hey, Sunny," he said. "Let's you and me blow this place, go to my place maybe, or yours. Get a little relaxed."

He smiled. It was a charming smile, but there was a tightness to it that I had not seen before.

"Not tonight, Bob," I said. "I've got an early day tomorrow."

"Too bad," Bob said.

"There'll be other times," I said. "You're quite fascinating . . . as you well know."

He grinned. The tightness had lessened. He took his wallet out.

"No," I said. "I invited you, remember?"

He paid no attention. He took a twenty from his wallet and dropped it on the table.

"You get the next one," he said.

"Okay," I said. "I had a very nice time, Bob."

Bob gave me a little thumbs-up gesture and left the

restaurant. I sat still and looked into my nearly empty wine-glass. Spike came to the table.

Without looking up, I said, "Keep playing the game."

Spike took the empty glass and the twenty, and walked back behind the bar. He poured me a second glass of wine and brought it back to me, and walked away. I sipped my wine and waited. Bob came back into the restaurant and walked to the table.

"Still here," he said.

"Still," I said.

"I seem to have misplaced my cell phone," he said. "Did I leave it here by any chance?"

"I haven't seen it," I said, and made a show of looking around and under the table.

"Maybe I didn't bring it," he said. "It's probably home on my bedroom table."

"I hope," I said.

"I'd leave my elbow laying around," Bob said, "if it weren't attached to my arm."

I smiled and raised my glass to him.

"Soon," I said.

He nodded and went out. I sat and sipped my wine.

After Bob had been gone for half an hour, Spike walked to the front door of the restaurant and went out to get some air. When he came back in, he walked to my table.

"No sign of him," Spike said. "How'd you get here."

"I walked over," I said.

"I'll take you home."

"I can go home alone, Spike."

"No."

"I have a gun in my purse, and some mace."

"I'll take you home," Spike said.

"He can shoot you from ambush just as easily as he could shoot me," I said.

"Easier," Spike said. "I'm a bigger target."

"I'll be fine on my own, Spike, really."

"I'll take you home," he said.

I knew he would, unless I ran for it. Which seemed undignified.

"Thank you," I said.

Spike was wearing a navy guayabera shirt. He went behind the bar and took something from under the bar and put it in his right hip pocket under the shirt.

When he came back to the table, I said, "Packing, are we?"

"No reason not to," Spike said.

Spike's black Escalade was parked in an alley behind the restaurant. Both of us paid a lot of attention to our surroundings as we went to the car. We were in the middle of the city, but it was late now, and there was very little sound in the alley. No one shot at us.

Once in the car, with the doors locked, we pulled out of the alley.

"He's not going to kill me," I said. "At least not yet. He's enjoying the relationship too much."

"I was watching him from the bar," Spike said. "He was posing for you like a peacock. First time I ever saw somebody strut sitting down."

"He was sexually aroused," I said. "I know it when I see it. I've seen it before in men."

Spike grinned.

"Me too," he said.

He parked the Escalade on the corner near my loft by a sign that said TOW ZONE: NO PARKING HERE TO CORNER.

"You can just drop me," I said.

"No."

"You're in a tow zone," I said.

"Find a tow truck at this time of night," Spike said.

We walked watchfully to the door of my building.

I said, "Thank you, Spike."

"I'm coming up," Spike said. "I want to see Rosie."

I nodded. Spike wasn't looking at me. He was surveying the street. My building door was locked. I unlocked it. I went in with Spike so close behind me that I could feel him. The big old freight elevator came down when I pressed the call button, and the doors opened. It was empty. Spike and I got in and went to the fourth floor. I could hear Rosie snuffling a little behind my loft door. I opened it. She scooted out and capered. I scooched down to pat her and Spike went past me into the loft. I always left lights on for Rosie.

When Rosie and I came into the loft, Spike had surveyed it and was content.

"Clear," he said.

"Oh, God," I said. "You've been watching those cop shows again."

Spike went to my kitchen and poured us two citron vodkas on the rocks, and brought them into my living-room area. He put them on the coffee table, took his gun from his hip pocket and put it on the coffee table beside the vodka, and sat on my couch. I sat beside him. Rosie wiggled herself into a comfortable position between us. Spike patted her absently.

"You're convinced this is the guy," Spike said.

"Yes."

"Okay, I don't have to prove anything in court. I'll assume you're right."

"Thank you."

"In which case," Spike said, "you are fucking around with a serial killer."

"I like to think of it as investigating," I said.

"And," Spike said as if I hadn't spoken, "he's almost certainly going to try to kill you sooner or later."

"You don't know that," I said.

"No, but it would seem stupid to work on a different assumption," Spike said.

"Yes," I said.

Spike's gun on the coffee table was a Browning nine-millimeter semiautomatic.

"Didn't you used to have a big old Army-issue Colt .45?" I said.

"Still do," Spike said. "But it's kind of heavy to carry."

I nodded. We both sipped our vodka.

"You're going to stay with this guy, aren't you?" Spike said.

"Yes."

"You think you keep flirting with him, he'll get so horned up that he'll confess?"

"Or do something that gives him away," I said.

"Like try to kill you," Spike said.

"I hope to prevent him," I said.

Spike put his feet up on the coffee table.

"He kills you, it won't make your father happy," Spike said.

"As I say, I hope to avoid that."

"It wouldn't make him happy if he knew you were taking the chance," Spike said.

"I can't worry about that," I said.

"The hell you can't," Spike said. "That's why you're doing it. You want to solve it for your father."

"I want to solve it," I said, "because it needs to be solved."

"It's been your father's albatross for twenty years," Spike said. "You're going to be the best daughter in the world. You're going to solve it for him."

"I . . ."

"You know this is the guy," Spike said.

"Yes."

"You want to roll him up, stop the killing."

"Yes."

"So you go to Richie's Uncle Felix, you tell him the situation, and you go home. In a day or two, Bob Johnson's in a landfill someplace, case closed."

"I can't do it that way," I said.

"Because?"

"It's not . . . it's wrong, Spike."

Spike smiled.

"You think?" he said.

"We don't need to get metaphysical about it," I said. "How about, it's illegal?"

"Lot of people have died waiting for the law to work. You sure it would be so immoral to have him killed?"

"I can't do it that way," I said.

"Because your daddy would never solve the case, might not even know that you ended it."

I sipped some vodka.

"How can you weigh more than the state of Montana," I said, "and be as smart as you are."

"It's a gay thing," Spike said. "Richie know about this?"

"No."

"You ever see him?"

"We're seeing each other again," I said.

Spike raised his eyebrows.

"What about the wife?" he said.

"Richie's moved out of the house."

"And I'm the fucking last to know?" Spike said.

"It's all been pretty sudden," I said. "And mixed in with this Spare Change thing . . ."

"And now is probably not the right time to talk about it," Spike said.

"No."

"Okay. But I got a little speech to give. I don't want you to die so you can be Daddy's favorite. Your father doesn't, either. And Richie doesn't, and neither does Rosie."

I nodded.

"But if it happens, I will see to it that Johnson dies shortly thereafter," Spike said. "If your father doesn't beat me to it."

"That would destroy Daddy's life," I said.

"Keep it in mind," Spike said.

"You'd kill him?"

"Maybe, or maybe I'd mention it to Richie and he'd kill him, or maybe he'd mention it to Felix. You die," Spike said, "one way or another, Johnson's gone in a New York minute."

"That's comforting," I said.

"Hell," Spike said, "Tony Marcus would probably do it."

"I'm hoping maybe to live," I said.

"I'd like to stick with you while you're doing this," Spike said. "But you're not going to let me."

"No," I said. "I do this for a living. How can I do this for a living if I have to be surrounded by a covey of protective thugs."

"Thugs?"

"However adorable," I said.

"I know," Spike said.

"You may be right, down the line," I said. "He may turn. No way to know. Since we don't know why he killed before, there's no sense trying to make any guesses about why he will again. I may not be what he kills. But if I am, he won't do it soon. Right now I am a rich masturbatory fantasy for him."

"He's probably home right now," Spike said, "snapping the carrot."

"'Snapping the carrot'?"

"You know," Spike said. "Sanding the bishop."

"God, Spike," I said. "You are such a smooth talker."

R ichie," I said.

Dr. Silverman nodded and looked interested. I wondered if she really was. How could she be? Clients coming in all day, talking endlessly about themselves, often boring, often saying things that she knows are evasive, failing to see the obvious, failing to understand what she probably knew about them the first day they were there but had to lead them to.

"We need to talk about Richie," I said.

She nodded as if she wanted to hear. I supposed that if she weren't interested, she couldn't do this. It was probably a little like me. I, too, liked to find out about people.

"He's left his wife," I said.

She nodded.

"He wants us to try again."

She nodded.

"I've told him I probably can't get married. He says he doesn't care. I've told him I can't live with anybody. He says that's okay. He said he loved me. He asked if I loved him."

She shifted her head slightly. It meant "Tell me more."

"I said I did."

She waited.

"He said it was a place to start."

"How do you feel about that?" Dr. Silverman said.

"I was hoping you'd tell me," I said.

She smiled and didn't speak. Had she ever had problems? Had she struggled with love and sex and things like that? It was hard to imagine.

"It's what he didn't do," I said. "He didn't ask me why I couldn't get married or live with somebody. He didn't say, 'What's wrong with you?'"

"Do you want to be with him?"

"I think so," I said.

"With conditions?" she said.

"Yes."

She nodded. She seemed relaxed and focused. Her makeup was understated and flawless. Her hair was in place without any hint of hairspray. Her clothes fit her perfectly. They were expensive and subtle, suitable for psychotherapy. Appropriate. Like her. Always appropriate. Did she ever get a stomachache? Was she ever scared? Did she always know what was what?

"What is wrong with me?" I said.

"I'm not sure *wrong* is the appropriate word," she said.

"Whatever," I said. "You know what I mean."

"I do," she said.

"Why can't I live with someone? Marry someone?" I said.

"How do you feel when you think about it?"

"Small," I said.

Dr. Silverman seemed absorbed by my answer.

"Talk about that a little," she said.

"I feel like, yes he loves me, but I . . ."

She waited. No hurry. She knew I'd get there.

"I feel childish," I said. "He's the adult, I'm the child. He loves me and takes care of me, but who and what I am doesn't matter."

She nodded slowly, calmly, just as if that weren't a silly way to feel.

"When you say *he,* are you talking about Richie?" she said.

"Any *he,*" I said. "Anyone I committed to exclusively. Any *he* that I lived with."

"Is Richie like that?" she said.

"Richie?"

"Yes."

"It's not so much what he does," I said.

"What is it, then?" she said.

"It's more how I feel."

"And what does he do to cause the feeling?" she said.

She was being positively directive. I must be on to something. I took a minute and thought about Richie.

"He's very self-sufficient," I said. "Very interior."

She nodded.

"He doesn't need to be taken care of much," I said. "He's a very capable man."

"So why does he need you?" Dr. Silverman said.

I looked at her for a moment. My mind felt blank.

"Need me?"

"Yes."

"To love, I guess."

She nodded. I was quiet. She was quiet. Somewhere I could hear the white sound of a central air conditioner.

"You know," I said, "when you asked me what he did, I told you what he was."

She smiled and nodded.

"He doesn't do anything, really, to make me feel that way," I said.

She continued to nod . . . pleasantly. She understood. She always understood. Even when I didn't. Did she ever misunderstand? Was she ever confused? Did she ever fuck up?

"It's not him," I said. "It's me."

"Yes," Dr. Silverman said.

"I suppose that's a good thing," I said.

She nodded again . . . neutrally.

"I've learned enough in here to know that I can't change other people. But I can change myself."

"If you wish," Dr. Silverman said.

"I'm not sure right now what I wish," I said.

"There's time," Dr. Silverman said. "We'll get there."

T aft University was the big school in the area. Its basket-
ball teams went to the NCAA tournaments. Its football
teams played in bowl games. Its campus was bigger than
some towns. It had begun life as a lovely rural campus with
a lot of red brick Georgian architecture and a green, open
campus. After World War II, veterans financed by the GI
Bill began to fill the campus, and when they graduated they
stayed, and Walford, where the university was located, began
to expand. The result was, sixty years later, that the town
was now a small city, and the university was a hodgepodge.
Some of the buildings looked like they'd been there since
the eighteenth century. Some of them looked like vocational

school projects. There was very little green remaining on the campus.

I drove out the fifteen miles from Boston on a fine Wednesday morning and parked in a faculty-only space beside the new library, which looked somewhat like a beached aircraft carrier. Inside the library, with the help of an alert librarian, I found a collection of college yearbooks dating back to 1911. I sat at a table, put the picture from Bob Johnson's bureau on the table beside me, and began to look at the yearbooks. If Bob Johnson was forty now, and all was normal, he would have graduated around nineteen years ago. I started there. Things had apparently been normal. Because he was there, with the rest of his graduating class. He had more hair then, but he was pretty similar otherwise.

He'd been on the yearbook staff, a member of an organization called the Social Committee, the chess club, and something called the International Relations Club. They all sounded to me like résumé filler. There were scraps of meaningless, to me, phrases beside the pictures of the graduating seniors. For Johnson they were ". . . last of the great ones . . . yes, we're related . . . farewell to Ike."

That was all there was, four years of college. A degree in accounting. I went through the yearbook page by page. There was a picture of the chess club, but no sign of Bob. There were pictures of the Social Committee, and the International Relations Club. Again, no Bob. In fact in the whole yearbook, though I couldn't make out everybody in all the pictures, I could find no other sign of Bob. In the faculty section was a picture of Bob's father, Robert B. Johnson III, professor of Business Administration. He was a pleasant, rather good-looking guy. Bob resembled him.

I kept at it. I went back four years, looking for Bob. I could find him nowhere in any of the yearbooks. He'd changed enough so that among the several montage pages of uncaptioned snapshots, he might have been there and escaped my eye. Nonetheless, it seemed as if he had been preparing even then to be a man of mystery.

When I got through, I sat up straight and arched my back a little and looked around. There were undergraduates of all genders in the library; some were studying, many were socializing. Many of the girls wore T-shirts and jeans. Which is what I was wearing. They weren't that much younger than I was. People probably thought I was one of them, Sunny Coed.

I went back to Bob's graduating yearbook and started looking for the woman. There was no special reason she should be in his college past. But there was no special reason that she shouldn't, either. It would have saved time and effort if I had looked for both at the same time. But when I'm really focused, I have room for only one item in the circle of my attention.

In the picture I had, she looked to be in her twenties, so she might not look so different than she would have looked in college. If she had gone to college. If she had gone here. If she had done so within the compass of Bob Johnson's tour. I went through the four years' worth of yearbooks page by page. It was slow and painstaking and boring. But it didn't pay off. She wasn't anywhere in any of the books.

I sat for a while. If I went home now, there'd be time to take a power-yoga class at my health club. Then home, a glass of wine, cook a small supper, some chicken, whole-wheat pasta, broccoli. I considered broccoli to be, for me, what spinach was for Popeye. . . . Or maybe she hadn't gotten to Taft until Bob was a junior, or a sophomore, or a senior. Maybe she would show up several yearbooks hence, if I stayed the course. Or maybe she had been here when he arrived and dropped out. I took a slow breath and got up and went for more yearbooks.

An undergraduate library assistant came by my table.

"Are you through with these, ma'am?" she said.

Ma'am?

"Not yet," I said.

"Wow," the kid said. "That's a lot of yearbooks. Did you used to go here?"

So much for Sunny Coed. I shook my head and the girl moved on. I got yearbooks on either side of Bob Johnson and looked not only at the graduation photos but at every picture I could make out. Clubs, snapshots, girls' field hockey. It was quarter to four in the afternoon when I found her. Maybe.

H er name is Victoria Russo," I said to my father. "She was two years behind Johnson at Taft."

We were having lunch at the No Name on the Fish Pier.

"Hometown is listed in the yearbook as Ardmore, Pennsylvania. But there's no one listed there now by that name."

"Alumni office got an address?" my father said.

"Wouldn't give it to me," I said.

"I'll get it," my father said.

"Get copies of the yearbooks while you're at it," I said. "Maybe we can find somebody who knew him."

My father nodded. He was eating fish chowder carefully,

not spilling any. It made me smile. He was a squat bull of a man but very fastidious.

"You get Victoria's address, I'll go talk with her," I said.

"Woman to woman," my father said.

"Girl talk," I said.

"You think the alumni office would be current on her?" my father said.

"They're more likely than the CIA," I said. "My alumni office knows every move I make."

"People can do wonders when they're chasing money," my father said.

"I've noticed that," I said.

"What do you think you'll get once we chase this woman down?" my father said.

"I don't know," I said. "But here's a guy that, as far as we know, never married. Does not, as far as we know, sustain a long-term relationship with anyone. Yet he's got a picture of a woman on the bureau in his bedroom."

"You think they had a relationship?" my father said.

"I have no way to know," I said. "Maybe they did. Maybe they still do. Maybe they never did but he wished they had?"

"Maybe," my father said.

"What about his father, anything on him?"

"Just that he died young," my father said.

"Date?"

"I don't know off the top of my head. But we have it."

"Cause of death?"

"Heart failure, if I remember right."

"Aren't all deaths because of heart failure, in some sense or other?"

"I think they were probably referring to congestive heart failure," my father said. "Why do you want to know?"

"Because I don't know," I said. "Any information is better than none."

He grinned.

"Right answer," he said. "I'll get you what we've got."

"Anything surfacing from that list of addresses?" I said.

"Not yet," my father said. "If he had any doubt that we suspect him, this should put it to rest."

"Because someone's bound to tell him."

"Yes."

"Doesn't matter," I said. "He has no doubt already."

"Won't do his business any good," my father said, "if these folks are clients and find that the cops are checking on their financial adviser."

"If he's the killer, it won't matter," I said.

"But if he's not . . ." my father said.

I looked out through the second-floor windows at the harbor and didn't answer. He was, I knew he was.

I t was another woman, this time. Near the Hatch Shell on the Esplanade. Wearing a tank top and shorts, and running shoes with pink laces. She lay on her stomach. There were three coins resting in the small of her back.

"Around five feet, seven inches," the crime-scene tech read off his notes. "They'll measure her exactly when we get her into the lab. Looks like about a hundred twenty-five pounds. Maybe, what? Thirty, thirty-five."

"Blue eyes," my father said. "Blond hair."

"Hard to tell about hair color, Captain," the tech said, "until we get a look in the lab."

"She may enhance it," my father said. "But she's fair-skinned. She'll be blond."

"Probably right," the tech said.

"Sunny," my father said, "let's talk."

I nodded. We walked to his car, parked among the other police cars, and got in. He started it up, turned on the a/c, and turned toward me.

"Notice anything about the vic?" he said.

"Third woman in a row," I said.

"Anything else?"

"She's my age, weight, and coloration," I said.

My father nodded.

"Have you drawn any conclusions from that?"

"It could be about me," I said. "Or it could be nothing at all."

"Fifty-fifty," my father said.

"Yes."

"I don't like those odds," my father said.

"I'm not crazy about them, either."

"I suppose you wouldn't back off of this thing," he said.

"Even if I would, Daddy, he knows my name. He knows where I live."

"You could come home for a while," my father said. "Lay low until we catch him."

"I'm the only thing you have to catch him with," I said.

"Then I'd rather we didn't catch him at all," my father said.

"And I live at home with you and Mother for the rest of my life?"

Behind us, on Storrow Drive, the traffic was backed up out of sight in both directions. Westbound, all the police vehicles had narrowed the roadway to a single lane. Eastbound, everybody was staring at all the police vehicles on the westbound side and trying to figure out why they were there. I could hear a traffic helicopter thumping dimly overhead.

"No," my father said, "you can't do that, can you."

"No," I said.

Around us the police were rounding up anyone they could find along the river. It was slim pickings. The Public Garden had been contained. But the parkland ran most of the length of the river.

"When you were a little kid," my father said, "your mother and I used to argue about whether you were old enough to go out alone, or cross the street alone, or ride your bike to school. I used to say, 'It's a risk you got to take sooner or later. She has to be on her own sometime.' And your mother would say, 'Not yet, not yet.' But finally it had to be, and off you went."

"And I survived," I said.

"Hell," my father said. "You flourished."

"Thank you."

My father was shaking his head slowly.

"I got you into this," he said.

"I was thrilled that you did," I said.

"And the only way to get you out of it is to let you do what you're doing and hope you survive."

"You think it's Johnson, too," I said. "Don't you."

"Yes," my father said. "So do Quirk and Belson. But we

have nothing. We haven't got enough to get a wiretap, a search warrant, enough men to really cover him twenty-four-seven. No fucking thing, nothing."

"He isn't dangerous to me yet," I said. "I said the same thing to Spike. I excite him too much. He's having too much pleasure out of me to get rid of me."

"So he's killing someone like you?" my father said.

"Maybe," I said. "Maybe a coincidence. You said yourself he's killed several men in a row."

"Maybe they looked like someone," my father said.

"I've read the files," I said. "They didn't even look like each other."

"I know," my father said. "I'm unhappy. I'm bitching. You think he'll call you again."

"Guaranteed," I said.

"You think he'll want to have sex with you?"

"I think he may be having sex with me now," I said.

"You think he'll press for the real thing?"

"I don't know."

"One promise," my father said.

"I won't be alone with him."

"Which will preclude sex," my father said.

"I hope," I said.

"Which might get him in gear."

"Yes. Does Mother know anything about this?" I said.

"No. Just that you're helping me."

"Let's keep it that way," I said.

"Yes," he said. "We will."

My father turned away from me and stared out through his windshield at the river. It was alleged to be swimmable again in some parts. I was adopting a wait-and-see attitude on that.

"Maybe I should stick around with you," my father said. "I could sleep on your couch."

"No more than you could walk me to school," I said.

"Yeah," my father said, "I know. I knew it when I said it."

Richie and I had a table by the window in the bar at the old Ritz-Carlton on Arlington Street. There was a new one up on Avery Street, which confused me, but I was adjusting.

I had a glass of white wine; Richie had beer. I smiled. We were both being careful. Richie caught the smile and got it.

"Don't want to be getting drunk amidst delicate negotiations," he said.

"Well, it's nice that we're careful, " I said.

"Maybe someday we won't have to be careful," he said.

"Or maybe we always will."

"Or maybe we always will," Richie said. "Doesn't matter."

"I don't want to be someone you have to be careful around," I said.

"You are who you are," Richie said. "Me too. We're smart. We can figure out a way to be with each other. What's Dr. Silverman say."

"She makes me wonder," I said, "whether I was the one mostly at fault in our breakup."

"She say that?"

"No," I said. "But talking to her, I'm beginning to think it."

"Probably don't have to decide that," Richie said.

"We need to understand more than we did," I said.

"We already do," he said.

"And more to come," I said.

We both smiled. I sipped wine. Richie drank beer.

"Phil called me this morning," Richie said.

"My father called you?"

"Yep. Said he understood we might get back together."

"He knew that," I said. "I already talked to him about it."

"He said if we were going to, now might be a good time."

"Because?"

"The Spare Change Killer," Richie said.

"Goddamn him," I said.

Richie smiled.

"I told him no," he said.

"You did?"

"I told him you wouldn't let me. I told him even if we

were together, we might never move in together," Richie said. "And if we did, it wouldn't be so I could protect you."

"You told him that?"

"Yes."

"What did he say."

Richie smiled at me.

"He said that he knew I was right. He said that you were pretty tough, and pretty smart, and there was no reason to think you wouldn't win this one. If we kept you from winning it, you'd never know you could."

"He said that?"

"Uh-huh. He said he thought maybe I could do something, without you knowing it, sort of, if we were getting together anyway. He said he was your father and he was scared for you."

"Yes," I said. "Of course."

"I'm scared for you, too," Richie said.

"I'd hate it if you weren't," I said. "But you understand, don't you, that I have to do this."

"Yes."

I leaned forward over the table and held both his hands in mine.

"You understand that if I can't be without you," I said, "I can't be with you."

"Yes."

"You really do?" I said.

"Whether I understand it or not," Richie said, "I know it."

"You didn't always," I said.

"No."

"How do you know it now?"

"I believe what you tell me," Richie said.

"God!" I said.

"Are you talking to me?" Richie said.

I smiled at him.

"No," I said. "That was an expostulation!"

"Wow," Richie said.

"It just sort of struck me," I said, "that of course you couldn't know what I needed until I did."

"This is true," Richie said.

Bob Johnson and I met for a drink on the patio at the Boston Harbor Hotel. It was late afternoon, not too hot, with a nice breeze off the harbor. I ordered a vodka and tonic.

"Damn," he said to the waitress. "That sounds good. I'll have one of those, too."

She went to get them. The place was public enough. Around us, people were coming in after work for drinks. They were mostly young people in good clothes. The tables were nearly all occupied.

"So, Sunny Randall," Bob said. "It's nice to see you again."

"And you, Bob."

"I see the Spare Change Killer has struck again," he said.

"Apparently," I said.

"Are you still working on that?" he said.

The waitress returned with our drinks.

"My father's still consulting," I said. "I'm still helping him."

"Ah, yes, Phil. How is Phil?"

"You know my father's name," I said.

"Sure," he said.

"How?"

I knew he knew it. We'd talked about it before. I was circling over the same territory.

"I read the papers," he said. "I mean, I'm sort of involved in this case ever since I got picked up in the dragnet in the Public Garden, you know? And, ah, met you."

Not quite the same answer as previously, but nothing incriminating.

"Phil is fine," I said.

"Good," Bob said. "Good, good."

He sipped his vodka and tonic.

"Boy," he said. "I'd forgotten how good those taste."

"Yes," I said. "They're nice."

"I imagine old Phil must be pretty frustrated by now, with this Spare Change case."

"I'm not sure my father gets frustrated," I said. "He was a cop for a long time. I think he just plows along until he gets what he's after."

"And if he doesn't?" Bob said.

"Then, I guess, he doesn't."

"Has he had many cases when he didn't?" Bob said.

A trio at one corner of the patio began to play "Green Dolphin Street." Piano, guitar, drums.

"Sure," I said. "All cops do. Lots of crimes don't get solved."

"Because the criminal is too smart for them?" Bob said.

"Often it's just that his luck is better than theirs," I said.

"But sometimes they get outsmarted," Bob said.

"Even then, it's more a matter of being less dumb," I said.

"Less dumb than the cops?" Bob said.

"There aren't a lot of criminal geniuses out there," I said. "Some criminals are just less dumb than others."

"But some of them must be smart," Bob said.

"Probably," I said. "Maybe some are so smart we never even know who they are."

"Except by their crimes."

"The real smart ones probably don't even let us know there's been a crime."

"Unless maybe they want you to know," Bob said.

He gestured at the waitress for another drink. She looked at me. I shook my head.

"The crazies are really hard," I said. "There's no logic to the crime."

"A person could want you to know about the crime without being a crazy," Bob said.

"Why?" I said. "Why would a person want that?"

"Might be a personal statement," Bob said.

"Of what?"

The waitress brought Bob another vodka and tonic. He drank some.

"Might be a statement of who and what a person is," he said.

"So what statement is the Spare Change Killer making, do you suppose?"

"Oh." Bob looked almost flustered and drank some more of his vodka and tonic. "We were just sort of talking in general, you know. I would have no way to know about a specific case."

I had pushed it too hard.

"Yes," I said, "the problem is for the cops, they are never talking in general."

He was bobbing his head slightly in time with the music.

"Yeah," he said. "Yeah."

There was a trace of red along his cheekbones, and I thought he might be breathing a little more quickly. He drank again. And when he put the glass down he was tapping his fingertips on the edge of the table along with the head bob in time to the music.

"What a great tune they're playing, Sunny," he said. "What is it? I can't remember the name."

"'How High the Moon,'" I said.

"Right," he said, "right. 'How High the Moon.' A jazz classic."

He swallowed the rest of his vodka and tonic. I still had half of mine left. He glanced at his watch.

"Holy moly," he said. "Look at the damn time. Sunny, I

gotta run. I got an evening appointment and I'm going to be late."

"Sure," I said. "I'll get the check."

"Oh, God bless," Bob said. "I'll get it next time."

"Excellent," I said. "That means there has to be a next time."

Bob paused and stared at me.

"You mean that?"

"Sure," I said. "We have fun."

"Yes, we do," he said.

He stood and smiled at me and said it again.

"Yes, we do."

Then he looked for a moment as if he were going to pat my shoulder. But he didn't. Instead, he turned and walked away.

"That," I said, "is a weird dude."

But I said it softly so that I was the only one who heard it.

Julie had a condo at the old Navy Yard in Charlestown. It had a modern kitchen and a big living room with a fireplace and a picture window. Ships sailed past within fifty feet. She and I were in the kitchen. I was opening a bottle of chardonnay, not my favorite. Julie was putting a big pan of lasagna in the oven.

"I got this at a place in the North End," she said. "But I'm going to claim I made it. So don't blow my cover."

"Okay," I said.

"I did make the salad," she said.

"Good for you," I said.

"Does the table look good?" Julie said.

"Sure does," I said.

"Thanks for doing this, Sunny," Julie said. "I know it's not your favorite thing."

"It'll be interesting to meet your friend."

"George," she said.

"And his friend?"

"Jimmy," Julie said. "Jimmy's in town from Milwaukee. Unexpectedly. And George said he'd feel like a third wheel without a date. So I thought of you right away. It could be really fun. It's been a long time since we used to double-date."

"As long as Jimmy understands that I am not planning to elope with him," I said.

I put the open bottle of chardonnay into an ice bucket and began to open a bottle of pinot noir.

"Is my bar okay?" Julie said.

She had bourbon and scotch, vodka and vermouth, tonic water, club soda, and a pitcher of still water. There were limes and lemons sliced in a glass dish.

"Sure," I said.

"What if they like rum drinks, or gin, or, you know, Canadian Club?"

"This is not a cocktail lounge," I said. "You're not required to provide all possible drinks for all possible tastes."

"I know, I know. I just want it all to be right."

"There are not many drinkers," I said, "who could not find something to choke down from what you're offering."

"I have beer in the refrigerator," Julie said. "Men like beer."

I nodded. The doorbell rang.

"Oh, God," Julie said. "They're here on time."

She took her apron off and hung it on the back of a kitchen chair. On her way toward the front door she paused at the front hall mirror and touched her hair.

The doorbell rang again. Julie opened it. I stood a few feet behind her, feeling awkward.

"Hello," she said.

The word came out slowly, as if it had several syllables. Her voice was an octave lower than it had been when she was talking with me.

"Hi, Jewel," George said. "This is Jimmy Hartsfield."

George looked at me.

"And you have got to be the legendary Sunny Randall."

"I am," I said, and put out my hand.

"Jimmy, Sunny," George said.

I shook Jimmy's hand. His clothes were good, beige linen slacks, a brown linen shirt. He was quite tall, slim, with a nice tan and a lot of thick, dark hair that showed the touch of an expensive barber.

"Really nice to meet you," Jimmy said to me.

We followed Julie into the living room. George had an arm around her. There was a small flurry while Julie got everyone seated. Drinks were organized and distributed. Hors d'oeuvres were passed. A ship eased silently past the big window, headed for East Boston.

"Is this a great view?" George said.

He was an inch or two shorter than Jimmy, and looked as if he had lifted some not terribly heavy weights. His fat was round and smooth. He smelled faintly of good cologne. He was wearing rimless glasses, and there was a fashionable hint of gray at his temples. Jimmy didn't glance at the window. He was looking at me.

"I like the view right here," Jimmy said.

I smiled modestly.

Oh, God, I thought. *He's one of those.*

Her initial round of hostessing done, Julie sat on the couch next to George. Jimmy and I sat opposite in matching armchairs. I tucked my purse down beside my right leg and sipped my wine. Julie was very close to George. As we talked and ate hors d'oeuvres, she rubbed his leg. There are few social events more tiresome than being on a blind date with another couple who are barely able to keep from having sex in front of you.

"So the client says to me, 'Jimmy, you're the only guy in the world I'd make this deal with. . . .'"

Julie's head was against George's shoulder. Her hand moved on his leg.

"You're the only guy in the world you'd let him make that deal with," George said to Jimmy.

Jimmy stood.

"You got that right," he said.

He went to the kitchen, got himself another bourbon and water, and poured me, without asking, another glass of white wine. He brought it back and set it on the coffee table in front of us, next to my other glass of wine, from which I had drunk maybe an ounce.

"Don't mean to push you, Sunny," Jimmy said. "But you know, things go better with booze."

He laughed vigorously. So did George. George put his arm around Julie.

"They surely do," George said. "Don't they, Jewel?"

"Things go best with you," Julie said.

"And in a little while," George said, "they're going to go even better."

George winked at Jimmy and me. Julie giggled.

Jesus Christ!

I felt like I should sit with my knees pressed together. From where I was sitting, I could see the clock on Julie's mantel. We'd been having cocktails for an hour. Julie was giggly drunk already. George and Jimmy weren't there yet. But they were blustering louder.

Jimmy was telling a joke.

". . . so the guy turns to his girlfriend and he says, 'I wish I was doing that.' And his girlfriend says, 'Go ahead. It's your cow.'"

Jimmy laughed loudly. George laughed loudly. Julie giggled. I smiled to be pleasant. I had first heard the joke when I was so young I didn't understand it.

"Go ahead," George said, and laughed again. "It's your cow!"

More laughter. Outside the big window, one of the harbor cruise ships went by, brightly lit, with people on deck looking at the waterfront.

"You can see why we love this guy, Sunny."

"How could you not," I said.

We discussed sports, money, Jimmy's business dealings, women both men had known, George's business dealings.

What a great time we were having. The lasagna had been heating in the oven now for more than two hours, and I held out very little hope for it. I appeared to be the only one hungry. I ate a few peanuts.

"Hey, Sunny," Jimmy said. "Lemme get you another drink. You're falling behind."

I had just begun my second glass of wine.

"No, thank you," I said.

Jimmy got up and went to the kitchen and poured some white wine in a highball glass and brought it back.

"Give you a chance to catch up," Jimmy said.

I smiled. On the couch, Julie and George had begun to neck. I tried looking at something else. Jimmy watched them for a while.

"Hey, Sunny," Jimmy said. "What's the most useless thing on a woman?"

"An Irishman," I said.

"An Irishman," Jimmy said. "Right, George?"

Jimmy looked at me.

"George is Irish," he said.

I nodded. George and Julie necked some more.

Jimmy gave me a wink.

"Boy," he said. "I wish I was doing that."

"Go ahead," I said. "He's your friend."

Jimmy looked a little confused. George put his hand under Julie's skirt. She pushed it away.

"George," she said. "Not right here."

George took his hand away and sat back.

"You know," he said. "That could be fun."

"What?" Julie said.

"All of us," George said. "You know what I'm saying, Jimmy?"

"Sure," Jimmy said. "A four-way. We haven't done that in a while."

"A what?" Julie said.

"The suggestion is," I said, "that George have sex with you and Jimmy have sex with me, and then we switch and you have sex with Jimmy and I have sex with George."

Julie sat up straight and stared at me.

"George and Jimmy?" she said.

"Whaddya think, ladies?" Jimmy said.

"It's a very good deal," I said to him, "for you and George. But what do Julie and I get out of it?"

"Whaddya mean?" Jimmy said.

"She's insulting us," George said.

"You want us to fuck both of you?" Julie said.

"Yeah," George said. "Together in the same bed would be best."

Julie edged back a little from George.

"Georgie," she said. "I can't do that."

"Sure you can," George said.

"Loosen up, ladies," Jimmy said.

"George," Julie said. "Stop it, please."

"Come on," George said. "Come on, stop with the coy shit."

He stood and started to pull her to her feet.

"Enough," I said.

He turned and stared at me.

"What?"

"Evening's over," I said. "Time for you to leave."

"You're kicking us out?" George said.

"I am."

"Like hell you are."

"I am," I said.

"Julie?" George said.

Julie had begun to cry.

"You better go, George," she said.

"Fuck that," George said.

"Goddamned cockteasers," Jimmy said.

"I think we should have our four-way whether they want it or not," George said. "Might be more fun anyway, you know."

I picked up my purse and stood. Jimmy stood, too, and stood in front of me.

"Just relax, baby," he said.

He put his arms around me and pressed me against him. I kneed him in the crotch. He yelped and staggered backward into his armchair and sat clutching himself.

"You bitch," he gasped. "You fucking bitch."

George turned away from Julie.

"What the fuck do you think you're doing?" he said.

"Get her, George," Jimmy gasped. "Show her something."

George took a step toward me. I took mace from my purse and sprayed him in the face. He stopped dead and buried his face in his hands, coughing and gasping, struggling to breathe. Julie was on the couch, sobbing. And I was pretty sure the lasagna was ruined.

I put the mace canister back in my purse and took out my gun. George had sunk back on the couch, rocking and gasping, his eyes shut, his face in his hands.

"That'll wear off in about forty-five minutes or so," I said to George.

Julie had moved as far away from George on the couch as she could get. She, too, had her face in her hands. She was still sobbing.

"Jimmy," I said. "As soon as you can walk, take your pal and get out of here."

"I'm hurting, bad," Jimmy said.

"That was the idea," I said. "If you don't get him out of here in the next few minutes, we'll call the cops and have them take you out."

"Cops?" Jimmy said.

"Assault," I said. "Attempted rape, maybe even make kidnapping out of the fact that you were asked to leave and refused."

I knew that wasn't going to happen, but I was pretty sure he didn't.

"We didn't kidnap anybody," he said.

"You have fifteen minutes," I said. "If you give me any trouble while we're waiting, I will shoot you in the head. If you're still here at eleven, I call the cops."

"Bitch," Jimmy said.

"Bitch with a gun," I said. "Your worst nightmare."

They were gone by the appointed hour. Jimmy was walking partly bent over, and George couldn't open his eyes yet, so he was hanging on to Jimmy. But by eleven o'clock they had tottered out the front door, and I had locked it behind them. In the living room, Julie was now facedown on the couch, crying very loudly.

The course of true love never did run smooth.

While Julie cried, I called Spike from the kitchen phone.

"Something has come up with Julie," I said. "I'll tell you about it later. But I think I need to spend the night here."

"And you want me to go over and stay with Rosie," Spike said.

"I do," I said.

"What if I have a date?" Spike said.

"Bring him along," I said. "When do you close."

"One," Spike said. "And, curses, I don't have a date. I'll go over now. Let Brigit close up."

"Thank you," I said. "You have your key?"

"Of course," Spike said. "I don't lose things like some of us."

"I don't lose things," I said.

"Oh, yeah," Spike said. "Where's your virginity?"

"Funny you should ask," I said. "I'll come home in the morning, and make us breakfast, and tell all."

"Okay."

"And be sure Rosie goes out before she goes to bed."

"Okay."

"And you know what to give her for breakfast if I'm not back yet."

"Okay."

"Spike, are you listening to me."

"Out before bed, usual breakfast. I'm all over it," he said.

"And don't be trying on my clothes while you're there, either," I said.

"Too tight," he said, and hung up.

I went back into the living room. Julie was sitting up now, on the couch, looking something close to tragic. Her lip gloss was smeared. Her eyes were red and swollen. Her nose was runny. Her eye makeup had eroded. She was breathing in a slow, shuddery way.

I was starving.

I sat down, cut a wedge of cheese from the serving board on the coffee table, took a few crackers, ate the cheese and crackers, sipped my crappy chardonnay, and waited for Julie to get her breathing under control.

"They've gone," Julie said finally.

"Yes," I said. "I watched their car pull away."

"Do you think they'll come back?"

"No."

"They were awful mad," Julie said.

"They are not tough guys," I said. "They just like to swagger in front of women."

"You think they're scared?"

"And humiliated," I said. "They'll probably get even by going and gangbanging some other woman."

"Can't you stop them?"

"You want to press charges?" I said.

"Oh, God, no," Julie said.

"Then no, I can't stop them."

"What will happen?"

"They don't know if we've told the cops or not," I said. "My guess is Jimmy will hightail it back to, where? Milwaukee? And George, without him, will just slink back home for a while and be grouchy with his wife."

"I don't want to see him again," Julie said. "What if he comes here? I mean ever."

"You know where his office is?" I said.

Julie nodded.

"Okay, I'll visit him tomorrow," I said.

"You'll visit him?"

"Yes."

"What if he does something."

"Doing something didn't work out terribly well for him tonight," I said.

"You weren't scared?" Julie said.

"Mostly I was mad," I said.

Julie blotted her nose carefully, with a paper napkin.

"I must look awful," she said.

"Nothing you can't fix," I said.

She nodded. We were quiet. It was quite late by now. No ships cruised past the big window, and the city lights across the harbor were more scattered. Julie was nursing a glass of wine. I poured myself a little. Mediocre is better than none. I felt a kind of post-adrenaline languor. I knew what it was. I'd felt it before.

"Men are lucky," Julie said.

"You think?"

"They don't always have to go around being afraid of getting raped or molested or whatever," she said.

"Because they are generally bigger and stronger than women?" I said.

"Yes. Unless we have a gun like you did, we have to do what they say."

"Men are afraid of each other," I said.

Julie shrugged.

"Most men are stronger than we are, but most men are weaker than other men," I said. "At best they have fewer people to fear, physically, than women, but there are still plenty."

"How do you know?" Julie said.

"I know men for whom strength and toughness and winning and losing is a daily issue," I said. "I work in their world, perhaps more than you do."

"It's your world, too," Julie said, "isn't it."

"I guess so."

"But you're so . . . female. There's nothing mannish about you."

I nodded.

"When I first thought about becoming a cop," I said, "my father told me that anyone can win a fight with anyone. In most cases it's only a matter of how far you're willing to go to win."

"You have a gun," Julie said. "I suppose that makes a difference."

"It's supposed to," I said. "But anyone can carry a weapon. The trick is will you use it. I will."

Julie smiled faintly.

"You did," she said.

"Yes."

"I'm not sure I could," Julie said.

"Most people don't know," I said. "And most people will never have to decide."

"You had to tonight, because of me," Julie said.

I smiled.

"I decided long before tonight," I said.

"It's why you do what you do," Julie said.

I raised my eyebrows.

"Because you can," Julie said.

This was a pretty good version of Julie. The one that kept me with her. Usually it was wrapped in the glib, overconfident, sexually aggressive, flamboyant Julie. The evening had undressed her, and what I liked to think of as the authentic Julie was visible.

"I'm such a goddamned stupid fool," Julie said.

"You're capable," I said, "of occasional misjudgments, I guess."

"It's more than misjudgment," Julie said. "I . . . I have no center."

I sipped my wine and didn't say anything.

"I mean, look at you. You know what you can do and can't do, and what you should do and shouldn't do. And you do it. And here I am thinking I'm in love with some goddamned pervert who's married to a client, and God knows what would have happened if you hadn't been here."

I thought about me, and Richie, and Jesse Stone.

"I'm not so sure how centered I am," I said.

"Well. What would have happened if you hadn't been here?"

I shrugged.

"Ménage à trois?" I said.

"Probably," Julie said. "And I would probably have let it happen, because I didn't know what else to do. . . . Are you actually going to see him tomorrow?"

"George? Yes."

"By yourself?"

"Actually," I said, "I think I'll bring Spike with me."

"You need a man?" Julie said. "What about all that I-am-woman-hear-me-roar stuff?"

"I'm not a feminist, Jule. If I'm anything, I suppose, I'm a pragmatist. I'm not trying to prove anything. I like things that work. Despite last night, I won't terrify George. Spike will."

"And you'll warn him not to see me again?"

"Yes."

"Or Spike will beat him up?"

"The threat may be implied more than stated," I said. "I'll play it by ear."

"And you think it will work?"

"You know Spike," I said.

Julie nodded.

"It'll work," I said.

I looked at my watch. It was twenty to one.

"Do you have to go?" Julie said.

Her voice was frightened.

"No," I said. "I'm going to stay the night."

"Here?"

"If you'll have me."

"What about Rosie?"

"Spike is with her," I said.

Julie nodded. She started to speak and couldn't seem to. Then she stood suddenly and put her arms around me and started to cry again.

"Thank you," she said. Her voice was hoarse. "Thank you."

I patted her back.

"You're welcome," I said.

39

Spike and I walked in to the Wellesley branch of Bay Colony Bank a little after ten a.m. The tellers were behind the long counter on the left wall. The suits of both genders were behind a railing on the right wall, sitting at big, dark wooden desks that radiated stability and trust. At the far end of the desk space was a conference room. It was empty. George sat at the desk three down from the conference room, talking on the phone.

"What's your job here?" I said to Spike.

"Look scary, say nothing."

"Correct," I said.

We went behind the railing and walked down to George's

desk. Spike was wearing a black do-rag, a black tank top, and little wire-framed oval-shaped sunglasses. He looked like a deranged biker. George hung up the phone as we approached and smiled at us professionally. Then it registered who I was and the smile went away. I pointed at him and then at the conference room and walked toward it. He looked uncertainly at Spike, then followed me to the conference room. Spike came behind him and closed the conference-room door. None of us sat. George stood on the other side of the conference table.

"What do you want?" he said.

I could see his eyes shifting regularly to Spike, who loomed in front of the door.

"The large gentleman behind me is Spike," I said. "If you go near Julie again, Spike will come and get you and beat you nearly to death."

Spike looked at George steadily.

"You . . . you can't . . ." George said.

"Can't what?" I said.

"You can't just come in here and threaten me," he said.

"Actually, we can," I said. "We're doing it now. We're in here threatening you."

"This is a bank," George said. "I can have the police here in like two minutes."

"Sure," I said.

I folded my arms and rested my butt against the conference table.

"What are you doing?" George said.

"Waiting for the cops."

"You think I won't call them?"

"I don't care if you do or don't," I said. "If you do, I wish to be here when they come."

George didn't say anything. His eyes kept shifting to Spike.

"You're both just going to stand here?" George said.

"Yeah," I said.

"I won't call the police," he said.

"And you won't bother Julie again," I said.

"I . . . look . . . I'm sorry about that. We were all a little drunk, I guess."

"I wasn't drunk," I said.

"Well, Jimmy and I, I guess, we had a couple too many."

"Where is Jimmy?" I said.

"He went home."

"Milwaukee," I said.

"Yes."

"You feel like going to Milwaukee, Spike?"

Spike shook his head no.

"Okay, then if Jimmy ever bothers Julie again, Spike will come and beat you up."

I could see the last breath of self-importance seep out of him.

"I won't bother her," George said. "Neither will Jimmy."

"And if either of you do . . ." I half turned. "Spike, will you hurt George if either of them bothers Julie?"

Spike nodded slowly, his gaze never moving from George's face.

"Badly?" I said.

Spike kept nodding.

"Honest to God," George said. "Nobody will go near her."

"Does your wife know about Julie?" I said.

"No."

"Keep it that way," I said, and walked toward the door.

Spike opened the door for me courteously and I preceded him out. Spike didn't come right behind me. I turned. He was standing in the doorway staring at George, as if he were memorizing every detail. Then he turned, and we left the bank.

In the car, I said to Spike, "What do you think?"

"He's kind of cute," Spike said. "What did Jimmy look like?"

"About as cute," I said.

"And they're not dating Julie anymore. . . ."

Spike grinned at me and moved his eyebrows up and down a couple of times.

"You and two straight perverts?" I said.

"They might want to change their luck," Spike said.

"Oh, ick!" I said.

"Hey," Spike said, "love is where you find it."

H ow often did Spare Change used to write you?" I said.
"The first time around?"

"At least one a week," my father said.

We were in the government center in the FBI offices, talking with Nathan Epstein.

"He's written me just once," I said.

Epstein nodded.

He was a thin man with not much hair. He wore round, dark-rimmed glasses, and he looked as if he rarely went outdoors.

"Maybe something else is giving him a charge," Epstein said.

"I think it's because we talk."

"You and him," Epstein said.

"Yes."

"Which would be Bob Johnson," Epstein said, "the guy you've been playing."

"Yes," I said.

Epstein looked at my father.

"Phil?"

"I think she's right," my father said.

"She probably is," Epstein said. "Say a little more about why he's not writing you."

"We meet for a drink," I said.

"In a safe place," my father said.

"In a safe place," I said. "We talk. He's flirted with me about the Spare Change Killer every time. Last time we talked, he did everything but tell me he did it. He doesn't need to write letters."

"Flirted?" Epstein said.

"I don't know a better word," I said. "It's like he's coming on to me, except it's about the murders. . . . No, that's wrong. It's not about the murders. He comes on to me about the killer."

"Which, in your script, is him," Epstein said.

"Yes."

"Okay," Epstein said, "so he likes to talk to you about himself."

"Yes."

"I'm told that a lot of men do that with women," Epstein said.

"They do," I said. "But they are usually not serial killers."

"Agreed," Epstein said. "But in your experience, when men talk about themselves, what are they doing?"

"Trying to impress me."

"You think that's what's going on?"

"Yes," I said. "In part. But it is also talking dirty, as if a man were going on about his sex life, excited to be talking about it in front of me."

"Sunny," my father said, "we may have to talk about your social life."

I smiled at him.

"The hell we will, Daddy."

He smiled back.

"Okay," Epstein said. "He's bragging about it and he's getting his rocks off talking about it."

"Like guys who expose themselves," my father said.

I turned in my chair toward my father.

"Yes," I said. "Yes. That's what he's doing. He's exposing himself to me."

"Most flashers don't want more," Epstein said. "Which may be good news."

"Or it may be that he goes too far and fully exposes himself," my father said.

"By actually confessing," I said.

"In which case he'd have to kill you to save himself," my father said.

"His letters to you, Phil, were, essentially, taunting," Epstein said.

My father nodded.

"His interaction with Sunny is, if I understand you right, Sunny, flirtatious."

"If you define it loosely," I said. "He seems to be trying to get us to agree on how special the Spare Change Killer is."

"So there's a *see me* in both approaches," Epstein said. "But with you there's the, shall we call it sexual, overtone?"

"Definitely sexual," I said.

"Do you think he wants to have actual sexual congress with you?" Epstein said.

"Sexual congress?" I said. "I didn't know FBI agents talked like that."

"Only if he's a Special Agent in Charge, and of Jewish heritage," Epstein said. "And in deference to your father."

"How many Jewish SACs are there, Nathan?" my father asked.

"One," Epstein said. "I think. Would you say that Bob Johnson's goal is to have sexual intercourse with you?"

"I don't know," I said. "At about the point when his sexual excitement becomes palpable, he ends the evening."

"Has he ever invited you home?"

"Yes."

"And you've declined."

"Nicely," I said.

"Has he ever asked to come to your home?"

"Yes."

"And you declined."

I smiled.

"Nicely," I said.

"But he knows where it is," Epstein said.

"He sent me a letter," I said.

"You in the phone book?"

"Yes."

Epstein seemed to turn this around in his head for a time. Then he started again.

"When you talk about palpable excitement," Epstein said, "what do you mean?"

I looked at my father.

"Palpable to me," I said. "His lips seem wet. His eyes seem to get bigger. His face seems to flush."

"Nothing as palpable as an erection," Epstein said.

My father groaned.

"None that I've observed," I said.

Epstein sat with his elbows on the arms of his swivel chair, the knuckles of his left hand pressed against his mouth. My father and I sat quietly.

"You got any thoughts, Phil?" Epstein said around his knuckles.

"The sex stuff, if Sunny's right, may be new. Maybe this is the first time he's had a woman he could flirt with like this."

"An attractive female investigator," Epstein said.

"Yes," my father said.

"Sunny?" Epstein said.

"Daddy may be right," I said. "But we're all guessing. Except about the attractive part."

Epstein nodded, still with his fist to his mouth.

"Guessing is all we know how to do, at this point," Epstein said. "I'll talk to the shrinks, see if they have anything to say."

"Quirk's got a couple on call, too," my father said. "Sunny will talk with them."

"Okay," Epstein said. "In the meanwhile, I would urge you to be very cautious with this man. We don't have a lot of history on this kind of perp. I don't think we know what he might do."

"I'll be careful," I said.

"I don't want him to kill you," Epstein said.

"Me either," my father said.

"Good," I said. "We're all on the same page."

41

My father called to tell me that Victoria Russo lived in Cranston, Rhode Island, with her husband, whose name was Leonard Mason.

"I'll go see her this week," I said.

"You could do it on the phone," my father said.

"No," I said. "I need to be with her."

"At least make an appointment," he said.

"I will," I said.

"Might be wise to keep the purpose kind of vague," my father said.

"I agree."

"Want to touch base with the Cranston cops?" my father said.

"No. I want to keep it informal," I said. "Do we have travel budget."

"To Cranston?" my father said.

"I might have to stay overnight."

"I have budget for that," my father said. "You can even buy a sandwich."

"Good," I said. "I'm not doing this for love, you know."

"Funny," my father said. "I thought you were."

"Do you have any more on Johnson's father?" I said.

"Bob Senior? I was over there reasoning with the alumni office. When I had persuaded them to cooperate, I went over to the Business Administration department. Not many people there anymore were there when Bob Senior was there. But the department secretary's been there since they named the university, and she remembered him. Secretary's name is Regina Hanley. Regina says that they got a call one morning from Mrs. Johnson Senior, says her husband never came home last night and she's beginning to worry. She says she calls but there's no one answering the phone. And she wonders if Regina could check his office. So Regina goes down to his office and it's locked. She knocks, and nothing, so she gets her passkey and goes in and there's Senior on the floor behind his desk, and she can tell he's dead. She says he just looked dead, and even if he wasn't, he's clearly not moving, and she doesn't want to deal with whatever was going on. So she closes the door and calls the university cops, and they come over with a paramedic unit, and take him down to the university health service, and the doctor there pronounces him dead and that's that."

"Heart attack," I said.

"Yep . . ." My father paused.

"What's the pregnant pause for?" I said.

"Effect," my father said. "Regina, clearly taken with me, despite her years, confides that she thought he had blood on him."

"Blood?"

"She says she can't be sure. She looked away as quick as she could after she found him on the floor. She found it, her word, 'repellent.' But she thought he was bleeding."

"Do people ever bleed from heart attacks?"

"Not that I know of," my father said. "Coulda banged himself as he was falling, I suppose, oozed a little."

I nodded.

"But the attending physician made no mention of it," I said.

"No."

"Nor anything in the campus police report."

"No."

"Was there an autopsy," I said.

"No reason," my father said. "Far as the Walford police were concerned, some professor at the college had a heart attack, and the college took care of it."

"Regina never said anything," I said.

"Not until she talked to me," my father said. "She wasn't sure what she saw. She found everything about it 'repellent.' She didn't want to get mixed up in it."

"But she told you."

"She found me reassuring," my father said.

"Daddy, did you flirt with her?"

"Of course," my father said. "Established investigative technique."

"Does Mother know?" I said.

"She suspects," my father said.

"Any sign of a weapon in all of this?" I said.

"No mention by anyone," my father said.

"How old was Senior when he died?" I said.

Again, there was a moment of silence on the phone.

Then my father said, "Forty-six."

"Jesus Christ," I said.

"That's just what I thought," my father said. "Here's another thing, may be nothing, but there was never another Spare Change killing until this year."

"That would be true of a lot of people," I said.

"I know," my father said. "But none of the others were the father of a suspect."

"Are you thinking that he might have done the first batch and his son might have done the second?" I said.

"I'm thinking everything," my father said. "Unfortunately, I can prove nothing."

"Father and son, twenty years apart?" I said.

"Maybe," my father said. "You always say I should think outside the box."

"If Bob Senior was Spare Change the first," I said, "it could be why he killed himself. If he killed himself."

"And if he was and if he did, it might tell us something about why there is a Spare Change the second," my father said.

"But no evidence yet, and half of what you're looking for happened twenty years ago."

"True," my father said. "And maybe nothing will pan out. But for the first time in twenty years, I have at least the beginnings of a theory of the case."

"Not a bad thing," I said.

"No," my father said. "Not a bad thing at all."

Vicki Russo had made us coffee. We drank it together in her living room. Her home looked as if it had been done by the staff designer at a furniture store. Everything matched. Nothing was very interesting. Vicki herself still looked like her picture. Her dark hair was shorter and had some highlighting. Her makeup was a bit more sophisticated. But, in her mid forties, she looked very much as she had when the picture was taken.

"Is Bob Johnson in trouble?" she said.

"No, no. Just routine stuff," I said.

I showed her the picture.

"This is you, is it not?" I said.

"Where did you find that?" she said.

"It is you," I said.

"Yes, college graduation picture. I never liked it."

"I know. I almost never like pictures of myself," I said.

We smiled. Two girls chatting.

"When is the last time you've seen Bob Johnson?" I said.

"You know, that's funny. I hadn't seen him since college, and then this year I saw him again."

"What was the occasion," I said.

"My husband graduated in the same class with Bob. I was two years behind them. We went back this spring for my husband's twenty-fifth class reunion."

"And Bob Johnson was there?"

"Yes," Vicki said. "He came over, and we talked for, oh, quite a while, half-hour, maybe longer. He has developed a very nice manner since college. Both Lenny and I liked him much better than we had when we were in school."

"Did you know him well in school?" I said.

"Actually," Vicki said, "I dated him for a while."

"How was that?" I said.

Vicki laughed.

"Uneventful," she said.

"What was he like?"

"He seemed very shy. He was nice enough, but there was no juice to him. About his only claim to fame was that his father was a professor there."

"Were you ever intimate?"

"Hey . . ." Vicki said.

"Sorry. It's something we have to ask everyone. It won't go any farther."

Vicki smiled and nodded.

"You're probably not a virgin, either," she said.

"Not for some time," I said.

"Yes," Vicki said. "Once. He was . . . not too good at it. I don't think he'd had much experience."

"He have trouble?"

"He wasn't impotent," Vicki said. "He got very, very excited, very little foreplay . . . and, ah, he didn't last very long."

"Don't you hate when that happens," I said. "Did he, ah . . . actually . . ." I made an aimless rolling gesture with my right hand.

"He did penetrate," Vicki said. "But briefly. I can't believe we're having this conversation."

"I know. It's awful," I said.

"Poor Bob," Vicki said. "He was so apologetic, like he'd done something terrible."

"Were you kind?" I said.

"Sure. I told him he was great. That it was fine. That I enjoyed it very much, that kind of thing."

"Did it make him feel better."

"I don't know. When a man finishes as quickly as he did," Vicki said, "he should know that it wasn't very good for the woman."

"Did you continue to date him?"

"A little. In truth, I wanted to let him down easy. You know, not stop right then and let him think it was his sexual failure, or whatever."

"That was nice of you. Were you intimate again?"

"No," Vicki said. "I think he was afraid to try again. And I didn't really want to. It wasn't just how quick he was. It was, I don't know. Something about how frantic he got when he did it, compared to how shy and sort of boring he was the rest of the time."

I nodded.

"How did he take it when you broke up."

Vicki tilted her head back and looked at the ceiling.

"He cried," she said.

She lowered her eyes to look at me.

"It was awful. He cried and told me he loved me, and begged for another chance."

"Chance?"

"To be better at sex," Vicki said.

I nodded.

"I was already friends with Lenny," Vicki said. "But we weren't, you know, a couple. But I talked with Lenny about Bob and Lenny said, 'You don't have to go out with some-body just because they want you to.'"

"And after you broke up with Bob, you started going with Lenny?"

"Yes."

"How did Bob handle that?"

Vicki smiled.

"Poor Bob," she said. "He used to trail us sometimes. Fol-low us around, you know? Watch us. Finally, Lenny told Bob he'd beat him up if Bob didn't stop."

"And Bob stopped?"

"He kind of had to," Vicki said. "Bob wasn't a very big guy, and Lenny played football."

She shrugged.

"So that ended it?"

"Yes," Vicki said. "I never had any more problems with him. I barely saw him in school, and once he graduated, I never laid eyes on him until last spring at the reunion."

"Where he was cordial," I said.

"Very. Really seemed to have turned out to be a nice guy, successful, easygoing. Really quite charming."

I nodded.

"When was the class reunion?" I said.

"Oh, beginning of June," Vicki said. "I could check back in my calendar if you want."

"Please," I said.

She went from the room, and in a few minutes came back into the room with the dates written on an envelope.

"So what's this about?" Vicki said after I put the envelope in my handbag.

"Just clearing up some details," I said.

"No, you're not," Vicki said. "I don't believe that. I'll bet you don't always ask all about somebody's sexual experiences on a routine case."

"I'll tell you some of mine," I said, "if it will make you feel better."

"Got anything good?" Vicki said.

I smiled.

"Well, there was this time in L.A.," I said. "On Rodeo Drive . . ."

"You're just trying to distract me," Vicki said.

"I am," I said.

"You don't want to talk about the case," Vicki said.

"This is true," I said.

We were quiet for a moment. Vicki fiddled with her now empty coffee cup.

"Rodeo Drive?" she said.

My mother invited me to lunch at her house to meet Elizabeth's fiancé, Charles Strasser. We ate in the dining room. Elizabeth, Charles, my mother, and me. My mother had made tuna-noodle casserole and served it with a side dish of tomato aspic on a lettuce leaf. There was a basket of brown-and-serve rolls, and butter in a cut-glass dish. Charles had brought some wine, and my mother was uncertain what kind of glasses she should use. She and I conferred softly in the kitchen. She had no stemware that matched, so we settled for lowball glasses. She also did not have a corkscrew, but we were saved by Charles, who had a Swiss army knife with a corkscrew attachment. He opened the wine expertly. When we sat down to lunch, I noticed my mother had quietly eschewed the wine, and provided herself with bourbon on the rocks.

The table had a white tablecloth on it and was carefully set with the silver she'd received as a wedding present all that time ago. Charles looked not so much appalled as puzzled when he sat down. He quite possibly had never seen a tuna-noodle casserole.

"This is a lovely-looking lunch, Mrs. Randall," Charles said.

The lying bastard.

"Thank you, Charles. I can whip things together pretty quickly when I need to," my mother said. "I had four tables of bridge here just two weeks ago and I fed them all, in jig time."

Charles smiled and nodded. He picked up his glass of wine.

"I'd like to make a small toast," he said. "To all the lovely Randall women."

He gestured with his glass.

"And especially to you, Mrs. Randall, the loveliest of them all."

My mother almost blushed. She raised her glance, sort of covertly. Since she was included in the toast, I knew she didn't know whether to join in it. She decided to, and drank some bourbon.

"It's too bad Daddy couldn't come," Elizabeth said.

"Oh, pooh," my mother said. "He and Sunny would spend all their time talking about those dumb murders and the rest of us could go fry fish for all they'd care."

"Murders?" Strasser said.

"I'm helping my father," I said.

"You're a police officer?"

"Was," I said. "Now I'm in, ah, private practice."

"You're a private detective?"

"Yes."

"This wine is fabulous," Elizabeth said. "Charles, tell us a little about it."

"It's really very drinkable," he said. "From Alsace. Ideal for a convivial lunch, I think. Especially with fish."

We all looked at the tuna-noodle casserole sitting on its hot pad in the middle of the table. If Charles had noticed my mother's bourbon, he pretended he hadn't.

"Well, it's fabulous," Elizabeth said. "You like it, Sunny?"

"Fab," I said.

My mother clearly wanted to get in on the conversation, but since she didn't have any wine to praise, she had to find another route.

"The tuna-noodle casserole," my mother said, "was always the girls' favorite when they were small, especially Elizabeth. Elizabeth used to beg me to make it."

"It looks delicious," Charles said. "Do you make your own noodles?"

My mother nodded enthusiastically.

"I boil them first," my mother said. "But about a minute less than they need, so that they can cook in the casserole without getting overcooked."

Charles nodded vigorously.

"And are they homemade?"

"Sure, I made the whole casserole this morning."

"And the noodles?"

I couldn't tell if Charles was merely making conversation or if he was busting her chops for his own amusement.

"The noodles?" my mother said.

As far as my mother knew, noodles came in a box. She'd never imagined someone making them.

"Mom uses Prince noodles," I said.

"Absolutely," my mother said. "I swear by Prince."

"They'll be fun to try," Charles said. "Anyone been to Tuscany?"

We hadn't.

"In the little local restaurants in Tuscany," he said, "in the villages, the chef will make his pasta right in the open kitchen as you watch, and serve it to you with vegetables fresh-picked from his own garden, and olive oil fresh-squeezed from his trees."

"I always add frozen peas to the casserole," my mother said.

"That sounds delicious," Charles said.

"You get to Italy much?" I said.

"I teach comparative literature," Charles said. "And I try to spend my summers enriching my understanding of other cultures. Literature is, after all, simply the voice of the culture."

I nodded. Elizabeth nodded. My mother stood.

"Have to check on the dessert," she said.

She took her glass with her when she went to the kitchen. When she returned, her glass was full.

"Well, I can't wait any longer," my mother said. "Let's dig in."

"I'll serve, Mother," Elizabeth said.

My mother seemed to have no objection. She handed the big serving spoon to Elizabeth, and Elizabeth began to put tuna-noodle casserole on our plates as we passed them. Sure enough, there were the bright green peas.

"So," Charles said. "Sunny, tell me a little more about yourself. You used to be on the police force?"

"Boston," I said.

"Like father, like daughter," Charles said.

"Exactly," my mother said, "like father, like daughter. What kind of work is that for a girl?"

"And you left?"

"I did."

"Because?"

"Too much protocol," I said.

"Yes," Charles said. "The academic world is similarly burdened."

"Is that a nice job for a girl," my mother said again. "We spent good money to send her to college."

"Oh, now, Mrs. Randall," Charles said. "In your heart, I'll bet you're pretty proud of her."

My mother's second bourbon was half gone. Elizabeth and I both knew what that meant, but any effort to slow her down would be loudly counterproductive.

"I'd be proud if either one of them gave me a damn grandchild," my mother said.

Elizabeth had grown slightly pale, I thought.

"Sunny paints as well," Elizabeth said to Charles.

"Really? Portraits?"

"Cityscapes, mostly," I said.

"Another self-indulgent waste of time," my mother said.

Her *l*'s were beginning slush on her, and she had a little trouble saying "self-indulgent."

"So, tell me, in your experience what would cause the biggest reduction in crime?"

"A cop on every corner," I said.

"A police state?"

"I don't know if that would be a police state or not, but that would cut back on a lot of crime."

"Don't you think eliminating poverty and racism would be more effective?" Charles said.

"Over the last five or ten thousand years, we haven't had complete success with that," I said.

"That's no reason not to try," Charles said.

"Had about the same success eliminating crime," I said.

"Again, that doesn't mean we can't," Charles said. "To think otherwise is to consign man to permanent imperfection."

"True."

"I'm not prepared to do that."

"Good for you," I said.

"Are you?" Charles said.

"Prepared to say that humans are imperfect?"

"Yes."

"I am," I said.

"That's defeatism," Charles said.

Elizabeth poured herself more wine. My mother drank some bourbon. Charles was aglow with the excitement of his intellection.

"You ever meet a serial killer?" I said.

"Whether I have or not," Charles said, "is irrelevant to the discussion."

"Let's not let experience cloud up the theory?" I said.

"Serial killers are an aberration. They're insane."

"That's often not the case," I said.

"Of course it is," Charles said. "Anyone who does what they do is insane."

I nodded. Charles was a professor with a Ph.D. He spoke several languages, had traveled widely in the world, and, as far as I could tell, possessed a brain the size of a Rice Krispie.

"I guess you're right," I said.

"No, no," Charles said. "Don't give up, I love intellectual rigor."

"Nope, I can't compete with you," I said. "Have you two guys set the date yet?"

"In the fall," Elizabeth said. "October probably."

It was quiet for a short time while we all sipped our wine and ate as much as we could stand of our tuna-noodle casserole. No one had as yet attempted the tomato aspic.

"Ship them all back to Africa," my mother said. "You want to solve the crime problem, send them all back where they came from."

Elizabeth looked as if something hurt. Charles's face had a sort of wooden stiffness to it. I sat and pondered, as I had so often. How much genetic responsibility did I have to my mother and sister? How thick was blood? At what point would it become acceptable to simply get up and leave? I'd never quite done it. Was this going to be the day?

My mother got up and took her glass to the kitchen. We were quiet. None of us had essayed the tomato aspic.

Then Elizabeth said, "Charles, tell Sunny about your book."

"I've just published a book on Dante's cosmography," he said.

"Gee," I said. "Congratulations."

"Pembroke University Press is bringing it out, and it's causing some excitement."

"I can imagine," I said.

"One reviewer said it amounts to a complete rethinking of *The Divine Comedy,*" Charles said. "A reconceptualized affirmation of the integrative accord between microcosm and macrocosm."

"Wow," I said.

My mother came back in from the kitchen with her glass full again, and sat down.

"How come no one's eating my tomato aspic?" she said.

B ob Johnson and I ate lunch together in a small café in the basement of his building. I was lunching with a possible serial killer, but at least there was no tomato aspic.

"That girl on the Esplanade," Bob said. "That was him, right?"

"Probably," I said.

"You getting any closer?" Bob said.

He was eating a Reuben sandwich. When I dined with Bob, I was never very hungry. I had a salad.

"I don't think so," I said.

We were outside on a little patio, below street level. The late-August weather was almost autumnal today.

"You know the cops are questioning some of my friends?" he said.

"Really?" I said.

"Yeah, isn't that cool?" he said. "It's like they had a list of people I knew, like I'm like a real suspect."

"I suppose," I said, "until they catch the guy, everybody's a real suspect."

"Yeah, but I must be more of a suspect than some people," he said. "I mean, they can't be questioning everybody's whole list of friends."

"You were at the scene of one murder," I said.

"A lot of people were," he said. "Nope, they're suspicious of me."

"Does that bother you?" I said.

"Bother me? No, there's no evidence. I think it's kind of fun."

"Fun?" I said.

"Yeah. It's like playing cops and robbers: exciting, but with no real danger, you know?"

"Because you didn't do it."

"Of course," he said.

So far everything we'd done to investigate him seemed to titillate him. Maybe I should push it a little. But if I talked about Vicki Russo, was I putting her at risk? No way to know. I didn't dare.

Instead, I said, "Talk to me a little about your father's death."

For the first time since I'd met him, there might have been a flicker of something behind his affable mask.

"I don't like to talk about that," he said.

I nodded.

"It must be hard," I said.

He nodded.

"You notice that the last three victims have been women?" Bob said.

"Yes," I said. "I understand your father died in his office at Taft."

"I told you," Bob said. "I don't like to talk about that."

I nodded and ate a small nibble of my salad. As always, I had dressed very carefully for Bob. Designer jeans, tight but not too tight. A pale green leather jacket over a white T-shirt. It would have been funny if he weren't what I thought he was. I gave more thought to my appearance at lunch with a serial killer than I did for a date.

"Of course," I said. "Do you think there's anything significant in the fact that our guy has killed three women in a row?"

"Maybe he's more interested in women these days," Bob said.

"How would that work?" I said.

"Why, Sunny," Bob said, "I don't really know. Even old Spare Change himself may not really know. I mean, you have things in your head and the next thing you know, it's influencing what you do."

"You think he has a girlfriend?" I said.

Bob did an elaborate shrug and finished the last bite of his Reuben. He patted his lips carefully with his napkin.

"How about you and me, Sunny?" he said. "Are we ever going to have a real date?"

"This isn't a real date?" I said.

"You know what I mean," Bob said. "Dinner, dancing, a walk in the moonlight, a good-night kiss, maybe more?"

"Slowly, Bob, slowly."

"Been burned before?" Bob said.

"Yes," I said. "You?"

He shrugged again.

"Let's just leave it that I understand," he said.

"Romance is hard," I said.

"You got that right," Bob said.

I was quiet, hoping for more. Nothing more appeared. We remained quiet while he gestured for the check and, when it came, paid it in cash.

"What a great day," Bob said. "Want to stroll down Commonwealth a ways?"

"Is it possible that your father might have committed suicide?" I said.

Bob stood up abruptly and walked away without a word. I was pretty sure he was not going for a stroll on Commonwealth.

Walford police headquarters shared space with the Walford District Court. The cops on the first floor, the court on the second. My father and I were in the chief's office on the first floor. His name was Wallace Spivey. He was tall and lean and scholarly-looking, with rimless glasses and gray hair.

"Wally and I used to share a patrol car," my father said. "Before he sold out to the suburbs."

Spivey smiled.

"Your father always insisted on driving," Spivey said.

"Still does," I said.

"After you called," Spivey said, "I went through what we

had on the Robert Johnson death at Taft. And what we got is nothing."

"What a coincidence," my father said. "That's what we got."

"I know the chief over at Taft," Spivey said. "Jerry Faison. But maybe better, I know the guy was chief when Johnson died."

"He used to be on the job?" my father said.

"With me," Spivey said. "But they made him a nice deal over there."

"Soft duty," my father said.

Spivey nodded

"And you think I sold out," he said.

"Can we talk with him?" I said.

"We can try," Spivey said. "I checked with him, and he said he had nothing to add to the official report."

"Maybe if we sat down with him," my father said. "And maybe we could find somebody who was on duty at the college infirmary when they brought him in."

"I asked Faison if he'd look into that," Spivey said. "I haven't heard back yet."

We drove over in Spivey's car to see the former Taft police chief.

"Name's Corey Hall," Spivey said as we pulled up in front of a white colonial house with green shutters.

"He doesn't know what we've found out from the infirmary people, does he," I said.

"We haven't found anything out that I know about," Spivey said.

"Mr. Hall doesn't know that either, does he?" I said.

"No," Spivey said. "He probably doesn't."

We sat on the back porch of Hall's house and had some iced tea that his wife made us. Hall was white-haired, though he was almost certainly younger than either my father or Spivey. He had a square build and a healthy outdoor look about him. At the foot of his neat back lawn was a vegetable garden. From where I sat, I could recognize corn, and tomatoes, and pole beans, and maybe summer squash.

"Don't know why this has come up again after all this time," Hall said. "Man was not conscious by the time we got there. Took him over to the infirmary, it was too late."

"They called it a heart attack?" my father said.

"Yep."

"You remember the name of the certifying physician?" my father said.

"Nope. Must be in the report, though."

"We'll get that," Spivey said.

"Folks at the infirmary seem to remember blood," my father said.

"Nobody over there even worked in the infirmary when this happened," Hall said.

"It's my understanding that there was blood," my father said.

Hall shook his head.

"Don't know nothing about that," he said.

"Why would there be blood on a heart attack victim?"
Hall shrugged.

"Ain't saying there was any. But if there was, coulda hit his head or something when he collapsed."

"So the presence of an abrasion would be in the report, too," my father said.

"There wasn't no abrasion," Hall said. "There wasn't no blood. I'm only saying if there was. Which there wasn't."

"You seem very young to be retired, Mr. Hall," I said.

"Can't say I'm feeling too young," Hall said. "But you're right, I took early retirement from Taft. Kids were on their own by then. Me and the missus don't need that much. I got a damned good retirement package."

"Do you remember how long that was after Professor Johnson's death?" I said.

"Hell, I don't know," Hall said. "A year, maybe longer."

"No hint of suicide surrounding Professor Johnson's death?" I said.

"Suicide?"

"Well, he died locked in his office. Was there any sign of a weapon?"

"If there was, it woulda been in the report," Hall said.

He looked at Spivey.

"What's going on here, Wally, this girl a cop?"

"She's working with her father," Spivey said.

"Well, I think she ought to go work someplace else and stop annoying me," Hall said. "And take you both with her."

A big springer spaniel with a gray muzzle came onto the

porch. He sniffed each of us carefully before he went slowly to Hall's chair and lay down beside it. My father put his iced tea down. He leaned forward in his chair and rested his fore-arms on his thighs and clasped his hands, and looked straight at Corey Hall.

He said, "I been a cop for more than forty years, Corey. I like being a cop. I like cops. I been friends with Wally Spivey for damn near as long as I been a cop. And you're a friend of his and you used to be a cop. I am willing to go a long ways for you if I need to. The death of Professor Johnson may, or may not, be tied to a string of serial murders that continues. The longer it goes unsolved, the more people die just for be-ing in the wrong place at the wrong time."

"You talking about the Spare Change thing?" Hall said.

"Yes," my father said. "If there's something you are not telling us about Professor Johnson's death, then a lot of people know what it is. The woman who discovered the body, the campus cops who showed up first at the scene, the EMTs, the people at the infirmary, the physician who certi-fied him. It's been twenty years, but unless they were real old, most of them will still be around someplace. It may take time, but we'll find them. We have FBI on this, and the Staties, BPD, half the city and town police departments in the state."

"Including mine," Spivey said.

"Do you think if there's something to cover up, every one of them will cover it up?"

Hall's voice was hoarse.

"Why do you think there's a cover-up," he said.

"Because I got a witness who saw blood," my father said, "and there's no mention of it in any of the paperwork."

Hall was silent.

"Phil's a decent guy," Spivey said to Hall. "You got something to tell us, we'll protect you. We'll keep you as much out of it as we can. But if you know something, you gotta tell us. We can't let this guy keep on killing people."

"How is the serial business connected to Professor Johnson?" Hall asked.

"We suspect his son," my father said.

Hall sat motionless in his chair on his back porch in the soft summer afternoon with his old dog asleep on the floor beside him. He gazed silently at his orderly backyard and the orderly garden at the foot of it. Tears formed in his eyes and slid onto his cheeks.

He nodded his head slowly. Nobody said anything.

"We'll protect you as much as we can," my father said.

Hall nodded some more. Still, he didn't speak. Mrs. Hall came out of the house. She looked sort of like her husband. Stocky body, gray hair, young face. Her movements were brisk, and her voice was cheerful.

"Anyone need more iced tea?" she said.

"No, thank you, Bea," Spivey said.

Bea looked at the group on the porch for a moment. Her gaze lingered on her husband, whose back was stiffly to her.

"Well, you change your mind," she said, "you just give me a holler. I'm in the kitchen."

"Thanks, Bea," Spivey said.

We were quiet for a moment after she went back in the house.

Then Spivey said, "What do you say, Corey?"

Hall nodded his head slowly.

"Yeah," Hall said. "He killed himself."

ere's how it went," Hall said.

He got up and walked to the end of the porch. The spaniel raised his head and watched him and decided they weren't going anywhere and put his head back down. Hall stared at his vegetable garden for a while, then turned and walked back.

"The department secretary called it in," Hall said. "One of my guys was there in maybe a couple minutes. It's not like we're all fighting crime night and day over there. EMT arrives about another minute later. There's a .38 revolver on the floor beside him, one round gone. Appears to have put it in his mouth and fired. Made kind of a mess. We got him to the infirmary, but we knew there was no point to it. He was gone by the time he hit the floor."

"So why didn't you call me?" Spivey said.

"Called the president first," Hall said. "Remember him, Larsen?"

"Perry Larsen," Spivey said.

"You know what he was like," Hall said.

"Attila is what I believe the faculty called him."

"Yeah," Hall said. "First thing he says when I tell him is, 'He had a heart attack.' I say a lot of people already know he didn't. He says, 'How many?' I say, 'Well, there's the secretary, the EMT, a doctor and a nurse at the infirmary. That's a lot of people.' Larsen says, 'I'll deal with them. . . .'"

Hall was silent for a moment, looking at his tomatoes ripening at the foot of his neat lawn.

"And he did?" my father said.

"He did," Hall said. "Including me."

"Wow," my father said.

"Larsen was a tough bastard," Hall said.

"Why the cover-up?" my father said.

"Good of the school," Hall said. "Larsen was trying to get Taft onto the elite college list. Johnson had just been voted teacher of the year. Got an award for some book he wrote. Larsen was afraid of what might come out if there was an investigation. I mean, he must have had a reason for killing himself."

"And Larsen didn't want to know that reason," my father said.

Hall nodded.

"Family know?" I said.

"Not from me," Hall said.

"Undertaker?" I said. "You have to do something with the body."

"Not my department," Hall said. "I cleaned it up at my end, and Larsen took care of the rest."

"This is pretty much a company town," Spivey said.

"Where is Larsen now," I said.

"Dead," Hall said. "'Bout five years ago." He smiled faintly. "Heart attack."

"You're sure," I said.

"I think so," Hall said.

"Bullet exit the skull?" my father said.

"Yeah. I dug it out of the ceiling."

"Anybody run ballistics on it?"

"No."

"You know where the bullet is now?" my father said.

Hall nodded.

"I got it," he said.

"How about the gun?" my father said.

"I got that, too. I was supposed to get rid of them, but a cop is a cop."

"Twenty years?" Spivey said.

"I couldn't throw it away."

"Anyone run ballistics on that?" my father said.

"No."

"Get them for me," my father said.

"There's something else," Hall said.

"What?"

"You'll see," Hall said.

He got up and left the porch. The spaniel watched him but didn't move. He was back in about a minute. The gun and the slug were in a big plastic Baggie. There was also an envelope in the Baggie. He'd known right where it all was.

"Can you do anything for me on this?" he said.

My father looked at the gun, and the slug, a little battered by its journey through Professor Johnson's head. But not so bad that they couldn't get a match off of it, if they had something to match it to.

"I got no problem with you, Hall," my father said. "I don't have to mention your name, I won't. I do have to, I'll mention only in the context of how helpful you've been. On the other hand, you conspired to cover up a homicide in Spivey's town. I can't speak for Spivey."

"Old news," Spivey said. "Larsen's dead. Who knows where any of the others are? I don't plan to reopen the case."

"Don't misunderstand me," my father said. "Sunny and I are going to crack this Spare Change thing, and if I have to throw you off the back of the sled, I will."

"But only if you have to."

"Only then," my father said.

"That's a better break than I deserve," Hall said.

"You got kids?" my father said.

"Yeah, four, all grown."

"Think of it as a break they deserve," my father said.

Hall nodded.

"Thank you," he said.

My father took the envelope out of the Baggie. He opened it.

There was a piece of white typing paper, the whiteness yellowish over time. My father unfolded it and read it and showed it to me.

"It was in his typewriter," Hall said.

The paper had three words typed on it in capital letters: ADIOS, CHICO ZARILLA.

I looked at my father.

"Is that name familiar?"

"I think so," he said.

"Bob Johnson's address book," I said. "The last entry."

"Yes," my father said.

"Has anyone talked with him?"

"We haven't found him," my father said. "He's never at his address. He has no answering machine. He doesn't respond to mail or notes on his door."

"Does he still live there?" I said.

"As far as we know."

My father looked at Hall.

"Anything else?" he said.

"No."

"You don't know anything about Chico Zarilla?" my father said.

"No."

"We'll do what we can for you," my father said. "You did what you needed to do at the time you needed to do it."

"I did what I was scared not to do," Hall said.

"Same thing," my father said.

The bullet came from the same gun as the last bullet used in the original Spare Change killings," I said to Dr. Silverman. "Which is the gun that was found with the body."

"Do you think that Professor Johnson was the original Spare Change Killer?" Dr. Silverman said.

"The killings stopped after he died," I said.

"And now you suspect his son of picking up the torch, so to speak?"

"The second round of killings started when Bob Johnson Junior became the same age his father was when the father died," I said.

Dr. Silverman nodded.

"And you're still seeing him socially?"

"Yes."

"Is that wise?"

"I don't know, I wanted to talk with you about him," I said.

"I am not a forensic psychologist," Dr. Silverman said.

"No, but I hold your opinion in high regard."

Dr. Silverman dipped her head slightly.

"He's very skittish about it, but he is clearly hoping to enlarge our relationship. Except the only real way he can be, for lack of a better word, flirtatious is to allude to the killings and our suspicion of him."

"And he's right, of course," Dr. Silverman said. "It's what makes him important to you."

"Does he actually think that because he's a serial killer, I'll go to bed with him?"

"He might think that you would go to bed with him because he's just like his father," Dr. Silverman said.

I sat back.

"Did you tell me that he had an encounter with his past just before the killings started?" Dr. Silverman said.

"Victoria Russo," I said. "What would be the connection."

"I don't know," Dr. Silverman said. "All we know is sequence, we don't know causality. But surely these killings mean something quite different to him than they do to you."

"Well, I suppose they do, don't they," I said. "It's funny, with something like this, you sort of accept the fact the killer is crazy, and forget that there's still a thought process going on, that he experiences the killings, and thinks of them in some way. I mean, he's probably not walking around thinking, *I'm a deranged murderer.*"

"It is impossible at this moment to know what he's thinking," Dr. Silverman said. "But these killings do seem to mean something to him, and from your experience, what they mean seems enhancing to him."

"I have taken him about as far as I can go," I said. "I don't know what to do with him. Do you have any thoughts?"

"I would like to know more about his relationship to his father and to Victoria Russo," Dr. Silverman said.

"Like what?"

"It might be useful if you could establish a correlation between their breakup and his father's death in any way."

"Or their unsuccessful sex."

"Unsuccessful sex?"

I told her about the hasty effort that Bob Johnson had made on Victoria Russo.

"He did penetrate," Dr. Silverman said.

"Yes, and ejaculated almost immediately thereafter."

"So he would have felt perhaps as if he'd failed?"

"She thought he felt that way."

Dr. Silverman nodded.

"What if I stopped seeing him?" I said.

"I don't know," Dr. Silverman said. "You are playing with very explosive material. It would surely be in your best interest to get away from it."

"I can't do that."

"I know," she said.

"I'm going to catch him. He needs to be caught."

"And you need him as an anodyne," Dr. Silverman said.

"Anodyne?" I said.

"As long as you have him to talk about, you don't have to face the hard things that need to be talked about in terms of Richie and your family."

"Or why I can't live with anybody," I said.

"Yes."

"Are you going to tell me I have to live with somebody?"

"No."

"I don't think I ever want to get married again, either," I said.

"I know."

"Do you think I should?"

"I think you should do what's in your best interest," Dr. Silverman said.

"Right now this is in my best interest," I said.

"Perhaps."

"You think I'm doing this just to dodge the issue?"

"You are a good person, Sunny. And a good detective, and you are doing what good detectives do. But things have more than one meaning."

"And as long as I'm caught up in being a detective, I don't have to talk about other things," I said. "To you, or to myself."

Dr. Silverman nodded.

"Richie, my family, that stuff."

"And you," Dr. Silverman said.

"We will get to that," I said. "But I need to do this first."

"And that need is one of the things I hope we can talk about," she said. "In the meanwhile, you need to be very careful. You mustn't let him kill you."

I smiled at her.

"That would not be in my best interest," I said.

On the website of somebody called Jimjam was a picture of Julie lounging in full frontal nudity on a couch, which I recognized from her condo.

"Oh, Jesus Christ, Julie," I said.

"It's Jimmy," she said. "George's friend. I know it is."

"He took the picture?"

"No, George did. But I know he gave it to Jimmy."

"How would I look this up on the Web?" I said.

"It says 'My Counselor: Nude.'"

I shook my head.

"You and Dr. Laura," I said.

"Like you've never posed nude," she said.

"In fact, I haven't," I said. "At least Dr. Laura can say she was young and foolish. This is a recent photo."

"How can you tell?" Julie said. "Do I look fat?"

"You just look like you," I said.

"You've got to make him stop," she said.

"There's more?"

"Yes. We took a lot of pictures." Julie looked out her window at the harbor. "Some of them quite graphic."

"I don't want to hear about it," I said. "And I don't want to see them."

Her gaze shifted back to me.

"Can you go out to Milwaukee?" she said.

"Milwaukee?"

"You, or send Spike, or both of you. I'd pay. He has to be stopped. . . . If someone recognizes me . . . if they find out it's a patient's husband . . . they could take away my license."

"You should have thought more about that when there was something to be done about it, like when you were flashing the camera."

"You and Spike could speak to him. It worked with George."

"George presented a possible physical danger to you."

"You know people, Richie knows people. We could have him killed."

"You mind if I click you off the screen?" I said.

She shook her head. I got rid of her image and looked up Jimjam on the Web.

"There are twenty-four thousand hits for Jimjam," I said. "How can we decide which one it is."

"We know."

"You know," I said. "You think I'd actually have someone killed on your say-so."

"My God, Sunny, you're my best friend."

"You got yourself into this mess," I said. "You'll have to get yourself out of it. An expert can probably track down the source of the pictures. Then you can get a lawyer, and maybe you can get a restraining order to prevent him from putting them out. Maybe not."

"You won't help."

"I am helping," I said.

"No," she said, "you're not. Lots of women allow themselves to be photographed nude."

"You're not a lot of women," I said. "You're a counselor, being photographed nude by the husband of your patient."

"I know. I know it was wrong."

"But you did it anyway? What the hell kind of counselor is that?"

"I'm not a trained psychiatrist, for God's sake," Julie said. "I have a degree in education. I took some courses in counseling and therapy."

"And didn't believe a goddamned thing you learned," I said. "And you presume to counsel people in trouble, based on a therapy you don't even believe in."

"I believe in it."

"You ever had psychotherapy?" I said.

"No," Julie said. "Not really. I mean . . . it seems so high a hill to climb."

I shook my head.

"People do what they believe," I said. "The rest is bullshit."

"But I've learned. If you'll just help me out with this . . . give me a chance to clean up my act."

"You've been spiraling down since you left Michael and the kids," I said. "I'm not going to help you go lower."

"You won't help me?"

"No."

"What am I going to do?"

"Probably get the lawyer first and he or she will find the computer guy."

"I could call Spike myself," she said.

I shrugged.

"You're a mess, Julie. You need serious psychiatric help."

"Don't you talk to me that way," she said.

"If you need a referral," I said, "I'll get you one."

"A referral? Me? You think I can't get my own referral?"

"You haven't yet," I said.

Julie screamed at me, "You holier-than-thou bitch, you have to help me."

"Can't," I said, and left the condo. She was still screaming at me when I closed the door.

Driving home, I thought about her. I was right. There was nothing I could do that would get her back to being Julie. I smiled a little. I wasn't proud of the thought, but in the nude she had looked a little chunky around the thighs.

Quirk and my father and I met in the Suffolk County DA's office in Bowdoin Square, with a senior ADA named Margie Collins. She was an attractive woman in her fifties with very blond hair, wearing a nice suit that fit her like an Armani. She had a couple of assistants with her, both female, who were so recently out of law school that they still smelled of diploma ink.

"Can we get a search warrant?" my father said.

"You bet," Margie said.

"What about the fact that I first came across this name illegally?" I said.

"When you burgled his apartment," Margie said.

"Fruit of the poisoned tree?" I said.

"Doesn't matter, the name was of enough significance that the police would have pursued it anyway and come to the conclusion that a search warrant was necessary."

"Inevitable discovery," Quirk said.

"Exactly," Margie said.

"Since I never heard anything about your illegal burglary, I will see no reason to mention it to the judge. We get into court and he's got a good defense lawyer, it may arise. If it does, we plead inevitable discovery. It'll stand."

Both her assistants took notes.

"How soon do we get a warrant," Quirk said.

Margie looked at her watch. It was three-thirty.

"Big case," she said. "High profile. Lot of pressure. I should have it by tomorrow."

"As soon as you can," Quirk said.

Margie looked at her assistants.

"Okay, Laurel. You and Kate get the process started. When you're ready, let me know and I'll start calling the judges who like me."

The two assistants hustled out with their notebooks. Margie turned to Quirk.

"You've given me the facts, Captain, or at least enough of them," Margie Collins said, "so that I can get you the warrant, despite Ms. Randall's banditry, but if you'd indulge me, do you have a theory of the case yet?"

"I'll let Phil answer," Quirk said. "He and Sunny have done most of the spadework."

"We're pretty confident that Robert Johnson Senior was

the first Spare Change Killer," my father said. "The evidence
all points to it. The gun, the bullet, the cessation of killing
at the time of his death. Probably even the suicide. Guilt
maybe."

"And the son?" Margie said.

"Sunny's spent a lot of time with him. She's convinced he
is Spare Change number two."

"He keeps talking around it when I'm with him."

"You're with him socially?" Margie said.

"Always in a public place," I said. "In fact, I'm scheduled
for lunch with him Friday."

Margie raised her eyebrows but didn't comment.

"You think she's right?" Margie said to my father.

"Yes," he said. "It's got to do with his father and a former
girlfriend and God knows what else. But yes, I think she's
right."

"Captain Quirk?" Margie said.

"Yeah. I believe her," Quirk said.

"I know you haven't enough yet to arrest him," Margie
said. "But have you taken steps?"

"Yes. We recently upped our surveillance. Four officers,
three shifts, twenty-four-seven."

"Is he aware of the surveillance?" Margie said.

"I'm sure he is," Quirk said. "We had him under some
surveillance before and he knew it, and shook us regularly.
He seemed to like it."

"And there's been no murders since this level of surveillance went into place?"

"No."

"That could be suggestive," Margie said. "Though hardly definitive."

Margie looked at me.

"You are a pretty tough cookie, Ms. Randall," she said.

"I know," I said. "I know."

My father and mother and I had dinner with Elizabeth and Charles in the beautiful high dining room at the Langham Hotel on Post Office Square. When the waiter arrived, my mother ordered bourbon.

"Do you have a preference, ma'am," the waiter said. "We have Wild Turkey, Jack Daniel's, Maker's Mark . . ."

My mother got a small, frightened look in her eyes. I had seen the look all my life. She smiled vaguely at the waiter and glanced sideways at my father.

"She likes Maker's Mark," my father said, "rocks."

My mother's smile became calmer and the little fear thing

went from her eyes. The rest of us ordered and the waiter went to get it.

She hadn't known what kind of bourbon she liked. If anyone had asked me I would have guessed that, but I never thought about it. And when she was asked a question she couldn't answer, she got scared; and when she got scared, she looked at my father. Who, in effect, rescued her.

The drinks came. Charles raised his glass.

"Family," he said, and we all drank.

I'd watched that same scene play out a million times. If she saw a mouse, if a pot boiled over, if one of us girls fell and skinned a knee, if the toilet wouldn't flush, or the stove wouldn't light, or someone asked her a question she couldn't answer, or gave her a direction she couldn't understand, the reaction was always the same—the sort of panicky screech that I had heard since I could hear: *Philll!* The screech was private, but the covert look she had just shifted onto my father was the public equivalent.

My father smiled as he raised his glass.

"Even this one," he said.

My mother frowned.

"There's nothing wrong with this family, Phil Randall, and don't you forget it."

He smiled at her. We drank.

I had seen all this before. Why did it so register now? I knew the answer to that. Most of my life, until now, I hadn't been sitting with Dr. Silverman twice a week, trying to figure out who the hell I was.

The waiter brought the menus and offered some explanations. Charles was impatient. My mother paid avid attention.

It must have been part of her charm. The helplessness. Nasty and demanding and bossy as she was, she was exotically dependent on my father. He could rescue her every day. Even her drunkenness made her dependent.

"I thought I'd buy us a bottle of wine," Charles said. "What kind of wine do you like?"

Again, the blank look, the enigmatic little smile of fear, the glance. Again, Phil to the rescue. All my life, I watched this all my life and never understood.

"I kind of like the Oregon pinot noirs," my father said. "But of course we'd defer to you, Charles."

Charles looked faintly startled. He hadn't expected my father to know anything more than white or red. It was such a Daddy moment. He always knew more than you thought he would. Talk about sailing and you'd discover he knew what a Marconi rig was. Talk about books and you'd find that he knew who Eudora Welty was. Talk about architecture and you'd find he had an opinion on Bauhaus. It was never clear how much he knew, or whether he was making a little go a long way. But he always knew something of which you were speaking. All the while looking like someone hired to keep order in a downscale nightclub.

"I was thinking about a French wine tonight," Charles said.

Which meant he probably didn't know much about Oregon pinot noirs.

"We can always drink an American wine," Elizabeth said. "Pick us some lovely French vintage."

"It is a night for a French vintage," Charles said.

My mother nodded vigorously.

"It is exactly a night for a French vintage," she said just as if she knew what that meant.

"You bet," my father said.

Elizabeth put her head against Charles's insubstantial shoulder.

I almost smiled. *Screw off, Daddy. I got somebody else now.* I understood Elizabeth. I should understand myself the way I understood Elizabeth. If we got our warrant tomorrow and searched Chico Zarilla's apartment and broke the Spare Change case and I went back to trying to put my life together, Elizabeth's relationship to Charles would last maybe another month. And then, when she wasn't fighting me for my father's attention, his professorial shallowness would become thunderous and she'd dump him, though probably not before she found somebody else to be with.

The sommelier appeared, and conferred with Charles in French.

I wondered as I sipped my martini if anyone had ever called Charles Charlie or Chuck. Several people in my father's circle called him Philz, and at least one guy called him Philzie. They had lived in different worlds, Philzie and Charles. Charles lived in a world of liberal-arts mumbo jumbo, where the idea was an end in itself. The accomplishment was having it. Considerations of execution were often dismissed with scorn. In many cases there was no execution. In its extremes, it was a world where being in love could be more important than making love. My father's world was full of things that mattered, often mortally, to people. What he did mattered. His decisions mattered. His successes were real. His failures were real, sometimes horrifically so. It made him understand that he mattered. And because he mattered, we mattered, mother and daughters, because we were his. It allowed him to feel deeply. He loved us because we were his. That was why he could love my unpleasant mother and my annoying sister just as much as he loved me, even though I was much more fun than they were. It wasn't about me, or Elizabeth, or even the dependent Emily. It was about him. We were his.

The evening pressed its way slowly to conclusion. My mother prattled. As she got drunk, the prattle got louder. Charles showed off for her. My mother flirted with Charles. Elizabeth and I competed. She blatantly, me subtly. My father showed every evidence of enjoying the evening. He was with us. It didn't matter what we did, or who we were. Or what we were. We were his. And in this part of his world, that was the only fact that mattered.

Maybe he was more like Charles than I thought.

We showed up in the South End at Chico Zarilla's condo a half hour before noon on the Wednesday before Labor Day. There had been a hurricane on the Gulf Coast, and we were feeling a modest spill out. The air was heavy. The skies were dark. There was enough wind to notice. And it was raining. My father was there, and Sergeant Belson with the warrant, a detective named Lee Farrell, a black guy named Trent something, and eight uniforms. The uniforms stayed on the street. The rest of us followed the warrant into the building. Zarilla's condo was on the ground level in a redbrick row house. We had already looked at building plans. The only exit was into a minuscule backyard that led to an alley. Four of the uniforms covered the alley.

Belson rang the bell. No answer. He rang again. No answer. He said loudly, "Boston police."

No response. Belson turned and walked to the front door and gestured at two of the uniforms. They came in with a portable ram and busted open the door. Everyone stood aside for a moment with guns drawn. The place was dark. Belson nodded and Farrell and Trent went in first. Belson followed. My father and I followed him. The uniforms held the hallway.

Somebody found a light switch.

I heard Belson say, "Jesus Christ."

The room was painted black: walls, floor, ceiling. On the wall, opposite the front door, was a five-foot-high black-and-white photograph of a man and a boy. The man looked just like Bob Johnson, and the boy would, too, in forty years. The man was wearing a dark three-button suit. The boy wore a child's version of the same suit. The picture had about it the clear sense that it was not recent. It was bland enough, except there was something chilling in the posed identity of the man and the boy.

"Bob Senior and Junior," I said.

Belson grunted. No one else said anything.

The condo was a studio, and not a big one: a bed, a bath, and a little kitchen. The shades were all drawn. Everything was neat. The bed was made with a white sheet and a plaid blanket. Besides the bed there was a low bureau, a desk, and a desk chair. One of the two detectives, when they came in, had opened the closet door and left it open. On hangers, still in the film packaging from the cleaner, were a suit, shirt, and tie like the one in the photo. There was nothing else.

"Anything in the bathroom?" Belson said.

"Hand soap and a towel, and two rolls of toilet paper," Trent said.

"That's it?"

"That's it."

"Nothing in the medicine cabinet?"

"No."

Farrell, wearing latex gloves, opened a bureau drawer.

"Vadda voom," he said.

We all looked. In the otherwise empty drawer were three .38-caliber Smith and Wesson revolvers. And seven boxes of .38 ammunition. Belson put his weapon away and put on some latex gloves. All of us did.

"Get some crime-scene people down here," Belson said.

Trent took out a cell phone and dialed. Farrell opened the lower drawer in the bureau.

"Scrapbooks of some kind," he said.

"There's one on the desk, too," I said.

Belson went to the desk.

"Along with a large jar of change," he said.

We all looked at the jar. The process was becoming eerie. The shaded room. The neat, barren quality of it. The overwhelming old photograph staring out at us, of the eerily similar man and child. The slowly growing knowledge of what we had found. We moved from revelation to revelation like tourists in the Louvre, staring.

"When you get through with the crime-scene call," Belson said to Trent, "get Quirk down here."

Cell phone to his mouth, Trent nodded yes to Belson. Belson looked down at the scrapbook on the desk.

"We'll back out of this," Belson said. "Stay put. Don't touch anything. Secure the place. Until Quirk gets here and the crime-scene people."

"Frank," I said. "We have to look in that scrapbook."

Nobody else said anything. Trent had gone to the hallway with his cell phone, as if he needed some routine gesture of politeness to offset the penetrating strangeness of the room.

Belson pursed his lips and breathed deeply and opened the cover of the scrapbook. I heard my father grunt. On the first page was pasted a large picture, taken at the Fenway crime scene and carefully cut from the newspaper, of me.

52

Quirk ran the gathering in a big corner room, down the hall from his office in police headquarters. Belson sat with Quirk. There was a big cardboard box on the floor between Quirk and Belson. The rest of us spread out around the big conference table. Epstein was there again, from the FBI, and State Police Captain Healy, the senior prosecutor Margie Collins, and Phil Randall, and his daughter.

"I want to nail this thing down, shut, airtight, leakproof, and done," Quirk said. "Before we open the gates and everybody comes in and tramples on it."

Everyone nodded.

"The scientists have been all over the room and its contents," Quirk said. "Here's what we know. The big photo on the wall is in fact of Robert Johnson Senior and Robert Johnson Junior. The scientists can date it. The room is full of the fingerprints of Robert Johnson Junior. As best we can tell, no one else has been in there."

Nobody said anything. We all wanted to hear about what was in the scrapbooks, and who the hell Chico Zarilla was. But we were patient. Quirk was never long-winded.

"There are ancient smudges that we probably couldn't match if we had to. There is also no evidence that the room was lived in. The stove shows no signs of use. There's water in the plumbing traps."

I looked at my father.

"Later," he murmured.

"The clothes in the closet have been laundered recently, and apparently regularly," Quirk said. "Place in the South End with walk-in service. Bed linens, too. Last record they have of him is twelve days ago. He picked up some cleaning and dropped some off. What he picked up is the suit, shirt, and black knit tie that you saw in the closet. He dropped off the same thing. Identical. Suit, shirt, black knit tie. Like the one in the picture. Forty-two regular. No labels. Don't know when or where they were bought. Only thing the scientists could tell us is that they aren't new."

"Could they be twenty years old?" Healy said.

His slim hands rested motionless before him on the table. The backs of his hands were freckled.

"Yes," Quirk said.

"Coins in the jar tell us anything?" Healy said.

"No," Quirk said. "Some could have been in circulation during the first killings. Some couldn't."

Quirk paused. No one said anything.

"Okay," Quirk said. "The guns. All Smith and Wesson, .38-caliber, two-inch barrel. All of them manufactured in the 1970s. None have been fired. The ammo in six boxes hasn't been used. Remington high-velocity, centerfires. Semi-jacketed, hollow-point. There are fifteen bullets missing from the seventh box."

"That gun holds five rounds," Epstein said.

"Yes."

"We have five victims," Epstein said.

Quirk nodded.

"He got rid of five rounds at the Public Garden," Epstein said. "One in the vic, four left in the piece he had to dump in the flowers."

"Means squat," Healy said.

"I know," Epstein said. "Just means he's got another gun maybe, and some ammo with him someplace else."

"It wasn't a complete toss," I said. "But I found neither in his other apartment."

Healy grinned at me. "That unexplained b-and-e that I know nothing about?" he said.

"That one," I said.

"God bless inevitable disclosure," Margie said.

I smiled modestly.

"He must have come by there regularly," Quirk said. "I assume it was one of the endless times he'd shake the surveillance. There's no mail collected. The room is clean."

"Maybe nobody wrote him a letter," I said.

"Light bills," Belson said. "Phone bills. Water bills . . ."

"Of course," I said.

"There was an upright vacuum in the closet," Quirk said. "The contents of the bag didn't tell us anything."

"Nice he was neat," my father said.

"There were twelve longneck bottles of Budweiser in the refrigerator," Quirk said. "Nothing else."

"Party animal," Epstein said.

Quirk looked down at his notes for a moment.

"And," he said, "there were these five scrapbooks."

They were numbered on the cover, in roman numerals, using what appeared to be black Magic Marker, number I being the earliest. The books themselves were standard scrapbooks, with pale gray covers. We passed them slowly among us, each of us taking as much time as we needed studying the one we had. Occasionally, one of us got up to get coffee. And stood to drink it. Nobody drank coffee at the table. Nobody wanted to be the one who slopped on the evidence. We had the Spare Change Killer or Killers in the room, in a sense. We were concluding a twenty-year investigation. And we had won. It meant something to everyone in the room, and it meant the most to my father. So we were very scrupulous, and surprisingly respectful, and very careful to go slow.

The notebooks were about two things: the life of Robert Johnson Senior, and the adventures of the Spare Change Killer. They were often the same thing. The clippings came mostly from the Boston papers, but occasionally there was one from *The Walford Weekly* or *The Taft Daily Chronicle*.

Robert Johnson named Lippman Professor of Business Administration . . . Prof. Johnson youngest chair professor in University history . . . a homeless man, identified as Roderick Fernandez, was found murdered . . . Johnson wins Helman Prize . . . The body of a young woman found this morning . . . Johnson honored as teacher of year . . . Spare Change Killer strikes again . . . Boston Police Captain Phillip Randall was named today to head the task force . . . Professor Johnson chosen commencement speaker . . . Spare Change Killer claims another victim . . . At his regular news conference, Captain Phillip Randall said . . . Professor Robert Johnson to Chair Committee on Diversity . . . Woman found murdered . . . Man found murdered . . . Woman found murdered . . . Professor Robert Johnson Succumbs to Heart Attack . . . Young black man murdered in Back Bay . . . Captain Phillip Randall, pictured left, with his daughter Sunny . . .

There were obits for Robert Johnson Senior, from the several newspapers that ran them. There were Christmas and birthday cards, and some photos. There were several pictures of Johnson Senior and Junior displaying fish they'd caught, paddling a canoe, playing catch, swimming together at an unidentifiable beach. The birthday and Christmas cards were from Senior to Junior and were affectionate. ". . . *No man could have a better son . . . to the best son in the world . . .*"

There was an eight-by-ten color photo of Robert Senior costumed in the Hollywood version of a Mexican bandit outfit, which had a page to itself. It was one of those pictures you can have taken in tourist spots: sombrero, crossed cartridge belts, two guns, and drooping false mustache.

I looked at my father. He nodded.

"Chico Zarilla?" I said.

"Seems a reasonable guess," he said.

There were photos as well of every victim, snipped from the newspapers. Both the victims of Spare Change 1 and the victims of Spare Change 2. And of course the picture of me. It had been a picture of me and Daddy, but Daddy had been excised. My picture as well occupied its own page.

It was late afternoon when all of us had read everything. The oddness of it was thick in the room. This was a group of very tough people, with long experience. But none had seen anything quite like this before.

"We got enough, Margie?" Quirk said.

"Oh, hell, yes," she said. "Christ, we could successfully prosecute him for being weird."

"Frank, we know where he is?" Quirk said.

"Haven't heard that we don't."

"Be sure," Quirk said.

Belson left the room.

"I'm scheduled to meet him for drinks tomorrow," I

said. "Late afternoon. Place called Spike's, down near the Market."

"I know Spike's," Quirk said. "What are you suggesting?"

"We could let him meet me. I could wear a wire. I could confront him with what we know, see what happened?"

"Why do we need to do that?" Quirk said. "We got him now."

"Because it may be our only chance to get any real information on how this worked. Father and son serial killers? Not together but sequentially?"

"We arrest him," Quirk said, "we'll ask him."

I shook my head.

"No," I said. "This is a game with him. He'll love the attention, just like when we first brought him in. He'll tell you what he thinks sounds good. You won't know if he's telling you the truth or not. He thinks we have some sort of relationship. When he hears it from me, and realizes I've been playing him, and knows that he's cooked, he might have the only genuine public reaction he'll ever have. I want to hear it."

"Because?"

"Because I haven't heard it. None of us has. And if we don't get it quick, we never will."

No one in the room said anything.

"We're all in the protect-and-serve business in one way or another, and we all care about that in one way or another. There's a bunch of Spare Change victims that we neither protected nor served too well. If we understand this guy, what made him tick, maybe we can protect some other people down the line."

"You want me to let him lose another day," Quirk said, "so he can talk to you over drinks?"

"You have him under close surveillance. Even if you didn't. This is too exciting for him. He's not going anywhere. You can fill every table and chair in Spike's with cops when I talk with him. It's our only chance to know."

Quirk looked around the room. Epstein shook his head. So did Margie, so did Healy. Quirk looked at my father.

"I can't make that judgment," my father aid. "I'm recusing myself."

Quirk nodded.

Belson came back into the room.

"Johnson's having lunch at Lock's with two suits," Belson said.

"Sunny wants us to hold off arresting Johnson until she's talked with him tomorrow wearing a wire," Quirk said.

Belson looked at me and back at Quirk.

"That's crazy," he said.

Quirk nodded.

"It's our only chance to know," I said.

Quirk looked around the room. Then he looked at me for a time.

"This," he said, "is pretty much your collar, Sunny. You spotted him early. You got us interested. It was you did the burglary that we don't know about. It was you that started poking around at Taft, and it was you got your old man poking around Taft. We wouldn't be in the room with this evidence if it weren't for you."

Nobody said anything for a time, including me.

Then Margie Collins said, "Martin. If you let her do this and it goes sour, it is your ass . . . big-time!"

Quirk didn't say anything. He kept looking at me. Everyone waited. Finally, Quirk nodded his head slowly.

"You're right," he said. "It's our only chance. You wear a wire. We'll bust him at Spike's."

Aside from Bob Johnson, Spike was the only non-cop in his restaurant. The two waitresses were cops. The business types having drinks at the next table were cops. And the drinks were tea and ginger ale. The happy couple having a sandwich just inside the door were cops. The guys sitting at the bar drinking what looked like beer were cops. Spike was behind the bar. My father was in the kitchen with Quirk and Belson. There were cops strolling by outside, and cops in cars down the street, and cops in the alley behind Spike's building. All of them looking like tourists, and people in from Framingham.

I was in the middle of the room, looking sophisticated and sympathetic in jeans, a loose-fitting beige jacket, a black T-shirt, and some soft, low-heeled boots that would permit me to jump around if I needed to. There was a microphone in my bra and a transmitter pack in the small of my back. I had my gun holstered on the left side, butt forward, under the jacket. Despite the massive police presence, I was uneasy, and it made me feel a little less so to have the gun on my belt, instead of in my handbag.

There was scotch on the rocks in front of me. I didn't want to drink. But I didn't want him to catch me drinking tea disguised as scotch.

Bob came in wearing a double-breasted navy blazer and a pink Lacoste shirt. There was a spring in his step. He was tanned and cheery.

"Sunny," he said. "This is great."

He sat down beside me, in the chair to my right. That was different. Usually he sat across.

"There's a ton going on," he said.

"Yes," I said.

Our cop waitress took his order for Tanqueray and tonic.

"They're following me," Bob said.

"Who?"

"The cops, who do you think? They are following me everywhere I go. They followed me here."

He looked around the room.

"They stayed outside," he said. "Afraid I'd spot them, I guess."

He laughed. While he was laughing, his drink arrived.

He raised his glass to me. I touched it with mine. He gave me a big, confident grin.

"To crime," he said.

He drank. I took a tiny sip.

"I sent you a present," Bob said.

"Really?"

"Yeah, in the mail." He laughed. "Which means maybe you'll get it this week."

"What is it?" I said.

"You'll see."

Bob grinned at me.

"It's a pretty interesting present," he said.

"How exciting," I said.

"I'm going out of town for a few days," he said, "and I wanted you to have something."

"What about the police," I said. "The ones following you. Will they object to you going out of town?"

It was as if both of us had entered into some sort of silent accord that I wasn't with the police.

"I can lose them," he said, "any time I want."

I widened my eyes.

"How?" I said.

"I know a building I can go." He was like a kid sharing a secret hideout with me. "It has a tunnel to the building next to it. I go in one building, out the side door of the next one, and poof, Bob has disappeared again."

"Wow," I said with my eyes still wide. "Where is this building?"

He grinned and shook his head.

"Can't tell you that, hon. It's a secret."

"I'd love to see it," I said.

"Maybe someday I'll show you."

I nodded brightly.

"Where are you going?" I said.

"When you get my present in the mail," he said, "you'll see."

His glass was empty. He gestured for another. Our waitress brought it. She was wearing a white shirt and black pants. Her gun was probably in an ankle holster.

"Bob," I said. "Will you be honest with me?"

"I'd never lie to you, Sunny."

We had arranged seating at nearby tables so that there was no one next to me and Bob. Nothing to inhibit our conversation. The waitresses didn't come by unless they were summoned.

"Tell me what you can about Chico Zarilla," I said.

Nothing changed that I could see, but something had. It was as if a door had shut.

"Chico Zarilla," he said brightly.

"He owns a condo in the South End," I said.

"South End."

"With a picture of your father in it."

Behind the bar, Spike was cutting up lemons and limes. The waitresses were hustling ginger ale and iced tea to a room full of undercover cops. My father was listening in the kitchen. But in the suddenly icy space around us, none of that seemed real. I had opened it. We were going to look at the gruesome thing inside.

"You've been there," Bob said.

"Yes."

Bob's gaze was entirely without meaning. It was like looking into the eyes of a frozen corpse.

"You and the police?"

"Bob," I said. "I am the police."

The silence around my table seemed impenetrable. I met his look. We didn't speak for a time. He looked slowly around the room.

"Talk to me, Bob," I said. "You can talk to me."

He kept surveying the room.

"Talk to me about your father, Bob. About the Spare Change Killer. Bob, talk to me about yourself."

Bob kept looking. Under his breath, he had begun to hum a song. I didn't recognize it.

"We have you, Bob," I said. "We know you did it. But I insisted on this chance to be with you. The chance for you and me to talk with each other. The chance for you to tell your side of the story."

He finished looking around the room, and looked back at me, and nodded slowly. There was a condescending expression on his face that might have included amusement. He continued to hum softly as he put his hand into his left-hand blazer pocket and took out two nickels and a dime and put them on the table between us.

The room seemed to organize around the coins. The cops stopped pretending they weren't cops. Everyone turned toward us. Bob saw it. It made him smug. He took another sip of his drink and smiled at me. He put his left hand on my shoulder, then brushed it against my hair for a moment.

"Sunny," he said. "Sunny, Sunny."

Softly, I said, "Bob, talk to me."

He took a fistful of my hair and stood and pulled me up from my chair and pressed a gun against my temple.

"I'll kill her," he said. "Anybody moves, I will kill her."

Time slowed way down, the way it does. Slowly, Bob and

I backed away from the table so that we were against a wall.
I could see us across the room in the mirror behind the bar.

"Phil," he said. "You're in here someplace, aren't you, Phil?"

All the cops had their guns out. Nobody fired. Four of
them, including our waitress, blocked the doorway.

"Phil," Bob shouted. "Come out, come out, wherever
you are."

My father came out of the kitchen and walked into the
dining area and stopped in front of us. At his side he had a
long-barreled .22 Colt target pistol. My father was a competition shooter. I recognized the gun. There was something
shocking in the familiarity of the object. It was incongru-
ously from home. My father didn't say anything. With his
grip on my hair, Bob had my head pulled back against his.
His right arm was across the front of my shoulder, clamping
me against him, while the gun was pressed to my temple. In
the mirror I could see him staring hard at my father.

"What are you going to do, Phil?" Bob said. "You can't
shoot, you might hit her."

Standing silently in front of us, my father moved slightly
to his right. Bob turned us slightly to compensate. My father
shifted into a competition stance, turning sideways, gun
aimed straight out from his shoulder, head turned so he was
sighting down the extended arm and over the gun sights.
Bob watched him.

"You've never caught me, Phil, and now you had to try
and trick me. You think I didn't suspect a trick? You think I
wasn't ready for it?"

We inched closer to the door. My father moved with us. In the mirror behind the bar it was like watching some sort of slow dance.

"I been ready for you all the time, Phil."

Bob giggled.

"Every day, Phil," he said. "Every step, you've been a day late and a few coins short."

Bob's eyes were fixed on my father. The gun pressed uncomfortably against my temple. His body, too. But he was watching my father, as if his spirit were lunging toward him. Despite the full-body contact and the restraining arm, it was as if I didn't exist, as if I were merely a towel he'd grabbed to cover himself. His whole existence was focused on my father. Phil and Bob, one on one. I was like an accessory object between them.

"Clear those people from the door, Phil," Bob said.

My father said nothing.

"What choice you got, Phil?" Bob said.

He inched us along the wall, holding me against him. As he moved, my father kept the target pistol up and leveled, aiming past me at what there was of Bob to aim at.

"Don't even think about it, Phil. Nobody's that good."

Bob giggled again. It was an awful sound.

"And you, at your age?" Bob said. "No chance."

It's not about me, I thought. *It never has been. For crissake, it's about my father.* Whatever sexuality had passed between us had been because I was Phil Randall's daughter. With the forearm of his gun hand, Bob clamped me a little harder against him. He kept me tight against him. I felt his pressure behind me. As we inched toward the door, my father kept the target gun leveled.

"We're going out, Phil. Nobody's going to follow. I'll drop Sunny Bunny off someplace when I'm clear."

"No," my father said in a voice like a razor blade. "You're not going out."

"I die, she dies, maybe a few others, Phil. But Sunny dies first for sure."

My father's gun tracked us like the pointer on a compass. The skin seemed to have stretched too tight over his face, and there were deep grooves around his mouth. In the mirror I could see Bob's eyes follow him. He seemed nearly entranced. His grip on me stayed tight, and the gun stayed pressing against the side of my head. But his soul was with my father. Bob's breathing was heavy in my ear. He pressed hard against me, watching my father, hardly aware that I was pressed against him, paying no attention to me, his accessory object.

Except that the son of a bitch was erect.

Phil Randall's daughter.

I had been fighting fear since he'd grabbed me. Holding myself still. Staying steady, watching developments, trying not to scream. Now I felt sick. This murderous pig was using me to protect himself, with no thought of me, and yet, rubbing against me, he was aroused. It was pornographic. It was an absolute denial of me as me.

The issue for Bob was not how much pleasure he got out of holding me captive, rubbing against my body. The issue was my father, not me. The threat was from my father, not from me. Bob was so engaged in his nonverbal interchange with that threat, and so obscenely unconcerned in whatever was causing his sexual arousal, that I could probably make a phone call and he wouldn't notice . . . or get my gun. . . . Quietly, I put my hand under my coat. I could see myself in the mirror. I could see Bob staring with smug intensity at my father. Quietly, I eased my gun out from under my coat. If Bob looked at the mirror, he would see me. If he saw me, he would probably shoot me. Didn't matter. I could not stand to be handled this way. I was willing to die more than I was willing to let this obscene son of a bitch use me. Carefully, I raised the gun. My father, of course, could see what I was doing. He didn't show it. His face stayed rigid. I put my gun close to my chest, pointing it upward toward Bob's arm that wrapped around my shoulder and held his gun to my head. It was an awkward position.

"Come on, Philly," Bob said.

His voice had an odd bubbly quality to it. As if there was too much saliva in his mouth.

"You know you're going to lose again," he said. "Do it with style, Phil. Clear the doorway. Or I will kill her right in front of you and the hell with the rest."

I heard myself say something to myself like *Here we go,* and shot Bob through the wrist. Bob grunted and staggered slightly and my father put a bullet through Bob's right eye.

Bob sighed and let go of me, and I dove to the floor behind a table. All the cops in the room started shooting the minute I dove, and Bob was hit probably twenty times by the time he fell. The silence after the gunfire seemed almost louder than the gunfire. The smell of the shooting was strong in the room. *Adios, Chico Zarilla.*

My father stepped over him and came to me sprawled behind the table. He put the target gun on the floor and sat on his haunches and began to pat my shoulder. He seemed short of breath.

"He had a hard-on, Daddy. He had a hard-on."

My father kept patting me.

His voice rasped when he spoke.

"Now he doesn't," my father said.

It was nearly three in the morning. Spike's was closed. The doors were locked, and there was a car outside with two cops in it, just to keep an eye. My father and I were having a drink alone, with Spike still behind the bar. I was having a double-sized martini on the rocks. My father was drinking scotch. My microphone was gone, and my battery pack. The lab was already processing the tape, making dupes. I still felt shivery cold.

"How could you have possibly decided to bring that target gun?" I said.

"I try to be prepared," my father said. "How come you had a gun under your coat instead of in your purse."

His breathing was calm now, but his voice was still hoarse.

"I try to be prepared," I said.

We drank. My father's face still looked tight. His skin was pale.

"Pretty ballsy thing," my father said. "Pulling your gun like that."

"I could see him in the mirror," I said. "He was fixated on you."

My father nodded slowly and drank some more scotch. It was restorative, I thought, for both of us. The jolt of the alcohol enlivening us, bringing us back from the dreadful place we'd been. Somehow it reiterated our humanness.

"What would you have done," I said, "if I hadn't pulled the gun?"

"If he took you out of there," my father said, "you were gone."

"What would you have done?"

My father drank again. His color seemed a little better.

"I'd have tried the shot," he said.

I nodded and drank again. I felt a little less chilled.

"I guess it didn't work out like I'd hoped," I said.

My father shrugged.

"We got him," my father said.

Spike came over with two more drinks, put them down, and left.

"I was hoping for more," I said.

My father nodded, turning his drink on the table in front of him.

"There's still the present in the mail," my father said.

"Think it'll be about the Spare Change killings?" I said.

"Everything was about that," my father said.

"I know. I think it was a good-bye present. I think he was running away."

"Yes," my father said. "I think when we put the twenty-four-hour surveillance on him, he knew we were getting closer."

"And what he'll send me will be some sort of farewell brag," I said.

"Be my guess," my father said.

He finished his first drink and turned to the second. So did I.

"If it is some sort of farewell horn blowing," I said, "I wonder how much we can trust it."

My father shrugged and shook his head.

"There may be no explanation," my father said. "What makes some of these guys so scary is that what they do often seems to them perfectly reasonable."

"I wonder how much he understood himself," I said.

"Not enough," my father said.

"Who does," I said.

My father looked into his scotch and didn't answer.

"Whatever he was, it was about his father," I said.

"And what in God's name was he about?" my father said.

I shook my head.

"Were you on the earphones?" I said. "In the kitchen?"

"Yes."

"Did you hear him humming?" I said.

My father nodded.

"Do you know what he was humming?" I said.

"'Three Coins in the Fountain,'" my father said.

"Oh, God," I said.

Spike came over to see if we needed more. We didn't.

"You got me covered, Phil?" Spike said. "They bust me for serving booze after closing time?"

"I can probably fix it," my father said.

Spike kneaded my shoulders gently for a moment, then went back to the bar.

"You all right?" my father said.

"Yes."

"You want to come home with me tonight?" he said. "Sleep in your old room?"

"And explain to Mother what I'm doing there?"

My father made a face.

"I could stay with you tonight," he said. "Couch would be fine."

"No, thank you."

"No need to be tougher than you have to be," my father said. "That was an ordeal to go through."

"We went through it together," I said.

My father nodded.

I said, "You are a rock, Daddy. Because you were there, I was less scared than I should have been."

He nodded again.

"You sure you'll be all right alone?" he said.

"I'm not only a big girl, Daddy. I have to be a big girl . . . otherwise . . ."

"Otherwise what?"

"Otherwise," I heard myself say, "I'll turn into Mother."

My father was quiet for a moment.

Then he said, "No . . . you won't."

woke up the next morning with a faint hangover, and a sense of loss. I'd worked with my father all summer on Spare Change, and now it was gone. I fed Rosie, and took her out and brought her back. I felt a sense of urgency and then remembered that there was none. I took a long, slow shower and washed my hair. I put on clean clothes. I ate breakfast. I drank coffee. I read the paper. The death of Bob Johnson hadn't made the early edition. I should have felt the luxury of no obligations for the day. I didn't. Instead, the day seemed ill-formed and long.

The mail wasn't due until early afternoon.

I cleaned my gun. I should have cleaned it last night when

I got home, but it was all I could do to feed Rosie, take her out, and then drag myself into bed. When I had the gun cleaned and reloaded, the light was right and I worked for a while on my painting. Brushwork often absorbs me. This time it didn't.

When the sun moved on and the light wasn't quite right, I cleaned my brushes and went to my health club. I did everything. Weights, treadmill, bike, stretching. My mother used to tell me that horses sweat, men perspire, and ladies glow. Halfway through the workout, I was sweating like a horse. The sweat felt good, as if it was somehow cleansing.

When I was through, I took my second shower of the day and put on my second set of clean clothes for the day.

When I got home, the mail had still not come.

I put my laundry through and folded it and put it away still warm from the dryer. Then I went downstairs and checked my mailbox.

No mail.

I went back upstairs and got Rosie and took her on her leash for a walk. I had my shoulder bag with my gun in it. For the first time in a while, I had no pressing need for it, but I had a license, and there was no reason to leave it home. Since Bob Johnson, the world seemed a somewhat more hazardous place than it once had.

We walked down across the Fort Point Channel and along Atlantic Avenue, through and around the moraine of the Big Dig. Rosie was, as always, adorable on her walk. Though she had some sort of genetic glitch that caused her periodically to stop stock-still and stare at nothing in particular. Sometimes she sat down. She'd always done it. I'd never under-stood it. Richie and I referred to the instances as "brain cramps." I had tried various cures, but the only workable so-lution was to stand still with her until she decided to start up again. It meant that a mile walk with Rosie took longer than most mile walks. Still, it was excellent patience training.

I knew I shouldn't get too excited about Bob Johnson's posthumous present. If it was something revelatory, it would be self-serving, particularly since Bob hadn't intended it to be posthumous. This wasn't going to be a deathbed confes-sion. In fact, of course, it could be a lovely framed photo of Bob himself, or a year's subscription to *Vogue.* And the Postal Service being what it was, it might not arrive today. Rosie paused in front of the Boston Harbor Hotel. I waited.

By the time we got home it had clouded up and started to rain. I checked my mail. The package was there.

It was a videotape.

When I sat on the couch to watch it, Rosie got up beside me. The first thing on the screen was an empty chair against a blank wall.

"Hi, ho, Sunny," Bob Johnson's voice said off-camera.

Bob walked into the shot wearing a dark blue suit with a white shirt and a pale blue tie. He was carrying a spiral-bound notebook. He paused and smiled into the camera, then he sat in the chair and crossed his legs. He held the notebook up.

"I have a lot of things to say, Sunny. So I wrote it down."

He smiled into the camera and waved the notebook a little. "Be sure not to leave anything out."

Beside me, Rosie stood up suddenly on the couch, turned around three or four times, and resettled against my thigh, in the same position, as far as I could tell, that she'd been in before.

On the television screen, Bob began to read from his notebook.

"By the time you see this and hear what I have to tell you," he said, "I'll be long gone and hard to find. Your father and the other cops are beginning to squeeze me. They follow me everywhere. Not that I can't get away from them if I need to. But it's becoming more laborious to do so, and it is hindering to my freedom."

Bob didn't read well. His gloss of charm fell away when he read. He looked up and into the camera every once in a while, as if he'd learned in some elocution school somewhere: Read three sentences, pause, look up, smile. It was graceless.

"So I'm moving on," Bob said. "But before I go, I'm going to tell you a story."

It was mid-afternoon, and raining pleasantly. The overcast outside had spread into my apartment. I would have turned on a light, but getting up to do so would have disrupted Rosie's nap. It felt a little cold for early September.

"I was an only child," Bob said, "and my mother was sort of nervous, and my dad was the one who had to do most of the parenting. He was able to do that because he was a professor and could be home a lot. My dad and I were very close.

My mother didn't like that. Now that I'm older, I realize that she was probably jealous. But back then I just knew she didn't like it."

The room was very still. Everything seemed artificial. I was looking at Bob Johnson and listening to him, and I had seen him die last night. It blurred everything. Reality, illusion; life, death; self, other; all seemed suddenly doubtful. I was aware of my breathing. I put my hand on Rosie, steadying myself as if I were dizzy. Her solid little self was comforting. Rosie was real.

"So one day, I was about fourteen, and my mother wasn't home. I went into my dad's study and he was dressed up like some sort of Mexican. Big hat, ammunition belts, like a bandito. I asked him why he was dressed up like that. He looked at me sort of funny. Then he went and closed the door, and sat down at his desk. And he said to me, could I keep a secret. And I said sure. And he said no matter what he told me, I had to promise it was a secret. Something only he and I knew. I couldn't tell anyone, including my mother. Just him and me. I said of course. So he took out his key ring and unlocked the bottom drawer of his desk and brought out a scrapbook and showed it to me. It was about the Spare Change Killer."

Jesus Christ, fourteen years old, high puberty.

"So I look at it, and while I'm looking at it, he tells me that he is really two people. He's him, Dad, most of the time. But sometimes he's also a guy named Chico Zarilla. And Chico Zarilla is the Spare Change Killer. I said what's the money for. He said the spare change stuff was just something to let everybody know it was him. It didn't mean anything."

I felt Rosie's muscular little certainty, solid against my thigh. She was snoring faintly. I kept my hand resting on her flank. Behind me, outside my window, the rain was persistent.

"You'd think I would have been shocked, wouldn't you," Bob said. "But in fact I was thrilled. My dad was famous. My dad was famous and mysterious, and dangerous. My dad killed people. And no one knew it but me. I didn't know what to say, so I asked him if he dressed up like Chico when he was being the Spare Change Killer. And he said no. He said Chico was the Spare Change Killer, not him, and Chico didn't want to call any attention to himself when he was doing it. So I'm really excited, and I want to keep talking about it, but I don't know what to say and I say, 'Is it fun?' How about that for a question, huh?"

Bob looked up into the camera in a stagy way, as if it said in his notes, "Look up at camera."

"And my dad says that's why Chico does it. It's fun. He likes it. And I so got it. I knew exactly what he meant. I knew it would be fun. And I say can I see your gun, and he says Chico keeps them here, in this closet, and he unlocks the closet door, and he takes out like a footlocker, and he unlocks that, and there's like a half a dozen guns, all the same, and a bunch of bullets, and I say are they loaded, and he says no. And he says would you like to shoot one? And I say yes, and he says okay, I'll teach you."

I picked up the remote and clicked stop and Bob's voice stopped and his image froze on the screen. Rosie opened a black, almond-shaped eye and looked at me. I patted her. With the tape shut off, I could hear the hushed sound of the rain coming down. I could hear it making a gentle noise on the big skylight over my easel. My head felt as if it were too full. The distant, ironic part of myself looked down at me, sitting alone with a small dog in a dim room watching this bland, bumptious monster talk about his father's serial feroc-ity, as if it were some sort of hobby, like fly fishing. I got up. Rosie looked at me with annoyance. I went to my closet and got out a pale green sweatshirt with a zipper front and put it on. Rosie thumped her tail in case I might be going to give her a cookie. Which I was. She took it promptly and chewed it briskly. I walked the length of my loft and back and went to the small bay where I had my breakfast table, and stood, and looked out at the red-brick neighborhood, gleaming wet in the early autumn rain. I looked back at Rosie. She was still lying down, but her head was up and she was watch-ing me.

"They're dead," I said to Rosie. "Both of them. They can't do these things anymore. . . . They're dead."

Rosie wagged her tail. I went back to the couch and sat down and picked up the clicker. Rosie readjusted herself against me, and put her head down and went back to sleep. I ran the tape.

"He taught me to shoot. In the woods, off the railroad tracks, in Walford. He never took me with him when he did the Spare Change thing, or Chico Zarilla did it. But he used to tell me about it after. We'd go in his study and close the door and he'd give me the details. On my sixteenth birthday, when we were alone, he gave me a picture of himself as Chico Zarilla. It was this thing we had . . . our thing."

Bob paused and looked down. I'm sure he had it in his notes: "Pause and look down." He probably had written "Pause dramatically."

Bob looked back up into the camera. "The year he died was a bad year," he said. "The woman I loved chose another man. Two very big holes in my life. But . . ." He shrugged. "Gotta keep going, right, Sunny? So I kept going, but last year my mom got sick, and before she died she told me my dad had confessed to her about Chico Zarilla, and then went to school that day and killed himself. The school covered it up and she let them. She didn't want people to know about him. She was worried his evil gene would get passed on to me. My mom thought like that, evil genes." He laughed and shook his head. "After she died, I went through the house and his office was like he left it. The guns were still locked up in there, and the bullets. I took them. . . . They made me feel close to my dad. . . . Then that same year I ran into Vicki again, the woman who left me for another man? . . . And I went home that night feeling really alone. My mother and father were dead. The only woman I ever loved was with another man. . . ." He leaned back in his chair and looked at the ceiling. He brought his eyes back down and looked directly into the camera. "But I still had Chico Zarilla," he said. He sat looking into the camera for a long moment, as if he wasn't sure what to say next. Then he smiled. "I'll miss you, Sunny," he said. "I really will."

He stood abruptly and walked out of the shot. The camera stared for a moment at the empty chair and then the screen went blank.